WOLF CREEK:
Murder in Dogleg City

Western Fictioneers Presents:

WOLF CREEK:

Murder in Dogleg City

By Ford Fargo

Western Fictioneers

*Beneath the mask, **Ford Fargo** is not one but a posse of America's leading western authors who have pooled their talents to create a series of rip-snortin', old fashioned sagebrush sagas. Saddle up. Read 'em Cowboy! These are the legends of **Wolf Creek.***

THE WRITERS OF WOLF CREEK, AND THEIR CHARACTERS

Bill Crider - Cora Sloane, schoolmarm

Phil Dunlap - Rattlesnake Jake, bounty hunter

Wayne Dundee – Deputy Marshal Seamus O'Connor

James J. Griffin - Bill Torrance, owner of the livery stable

Jerry Guin - Deputy Marshal Quint Croy

Douglas Hirt - Marcus Sublette, schoolteacher and headmaster

L. J. Martin - Angus "Spike" Sweeney, blacksmith

Matthew P. Mayo - Rupert "Rupe" Tingley, town drunk

Kerry Newcomb - James Reginald de Courcey, artist with a secret

Cheryl Pierson - Derrick McCain, farmer

Robert J. Randisi - Dave Benteen, gunsmith

James Reasoner - G.W. Satterlee, county sheriff

Frank Roderus - John Nix, barber

Troy D. Smith - Charley Blackfeather, scout; Sam Gardner, town marshal

Clay More - Logan Munro, town doctor

Chuck Tyrell - Billy Below, young cowboy; Sam Jones, gambler

Jackson Lowry - Wilson "Wil" Marsh, photographer

L. J. Washburn - Ira Breedlove, owner of the Wolf's Den Saloon

Matthew Pizzolato - Wesley Quaid, drifter

Appearing as Ford Fargo in this episode:

L. J. Washburn (Ira Breedlove)- Prologue, Chapter 4

Jerry Guin (Deputy Quint Croy)- Chapter 1

Chuck Tyrell (Samuel Jones / Philippe Beaumont)-
Chapter 2, interlude

Troy D. Smith (Marshal Sam Gardner)- Chapter 3

Matthew P. Mayo (Rupe Tingley)- Chapter 5

Phil Dunlap (Rattlesnake Jake)- Chapter 6

INTRODUCTION

In Wolf Creek, everyone has a secret.

That includes our author, Ford Fargo—but we have decided to make his identity an *open* secret. Ford Fargo is the "house name" of Western Fictioneers—the only professional writers' organization devoted exclusively to the traditional western, and which includes many of the top names working in the genre today.

Wolf Creek is our playground.

It is a fictional town in 1871 Kansas. Each WF member participating in our project has created his or her own "main character," and each chapter in every volume of our series will be primarily written by a different writer, with their own townsperson serving as the principal point-of-view character for that chapter (or two, sometimes.) It will be sort of like a television series with a large ensemble cast; it will be like one of those Massive Multi-player Role-playing Games you can immerse yourself in online. And it is like nothing that has ever been done in the western genre before.

You can explore our town and its citizens at our website if you wish:

http://wolfcreekkansas.yolasite.com

Or you can simply turn this page, and step into the dusty streets of Wolf Creek.

Just be careful. It's a nice place to visit, but you wouldn't want to die there.

Troy D. Smith
President, Western Fictioneers
Wolf Creek series editor

Wolf Creek: Murder in Dogleg City

MURDER IN DOGLEG CITY

PROLOGUE

Laird Jenkins had been in so many saloons, gambling dens, and houses of ill repute across the West that he couldn't even begin to remember all of them. Sometimes it seemed to him that he had spent his entire life breathing in the distinctive yet dubious perfume blended from tobacco smoke, stale beer, whiskey, piss, unwashed human flesh, bay rum, and cheap lilac water.

One thing he knew: the dens of iniquity here in Dogleg City, the less savory area of the settlement known as Wolf Creek, weren't any different from the ones he had visited elsewhere, with one or two exceptions.

The place he was in at the moment, Asa's Saloon, was one of those exceptions. It was owned by a black man, something you didn't see every day. Many of the clientele were black as well, but not all—there were a handful of Mexicans and a few white men who looked down on their luck. Not the sort of place Laird would normally choose to drink in, but he wasn't really there to drink. He was there to do a little business with Asa Pepper. That business wasn't concluded yet, but Laird thought he had made a good start on it.

Without saying good night to anyone – there wasn't anyone in here that he would want to strike up a social conversation with, as Asa's customers tended to be the dregs of the town – Laird left the saloon. He paused on the boardwalk just outside to take a deep breath of the night air and clear some of the saloon fumes from his lungs. He was about to head toward the Imperial Hotel, ready to turn in for the night, when an overpowering urge struck him. He turned the other way, toward the nearby alley, and started fumbling with the buttons of his fly.

Damn, he told himself, he wasn't old enough to be plagued like this. He ought to have a few years left, at least, before he started having to hurry these things or else he'd piss his britches.

The darkness of the alley folded around him. He got himself set, ready to relieve his bladder. And then, wouldn't you know it, the blasted thing went balky on him and refused to do anything.

With that to worry him, he almost didn't hear the faint noise of someone moving behind him. Laird didn't particularly like the idea of being disturbed at his personal business like this, and he knew as well that robbers often lurked in alleys near saloons, lying in wait for unwary drunks. His hand moved slightly toward the butt of the Colt on his hip.

But maybe it was nothing. A cat or a rat. Or maybe Asa Pepper had followed him from the saloon, deciding that he wanted to hear more of what Laird had to say about how they could both make some money.

"Mister Pepper?" Laird said without looking behind him. "Is that—"

The muzzle flash split the darkness. A blink of orange flame, there and then gone, and as it lit up the alley something smashed into Laird's back, a hammer-blow almost perfectly centered between his shoulder blades. It drove him forward off his feet. His face smashed into the hard-packed dirt of the alley floor. A fierce pain expanded through him, followed by an even more terrifying numbness. In that brief moment while Laird's muscles still worked, he managed to roll onto his back. Dying in an alley behind a saloon was bad enough. Dying with his face in the dirt and shit and trash of that alley was worse.

Laird tried and failed to draw air into his lungs. Everything was slipping away from him, and he wished he could breathe in that heady saloon fragrance once again, just one more time, just . . .

CHAPTER ONE

It was not long past daylight. The morning sun slanted low over the rooftops of the buildings, layering the town with its early light. Deputy Marshal Quint Croy sat at his desk in the marshal's office—it had been a long night.

Quint was twenty-five years old, tall, with sandy hair and steady gray eyes. He had a prominent, beaklike nose—a frequent target for punches, but it had survived many assaults. His manner of dress and the way he carried himself indicated he had spent more time as a cowboy than a lawman.

And indeed he had. Quint Croy had worked as a drover for six years before he came to Wolf Creek. He had been on four trail drives from Texas to Kansas—the final one had ended tragically, for one of his best friends had been shot dead in a low class Abilene saloon, in a meaningless fracas.

Another saloon patron, insulted over an imagined slight, had drawn on the unfortunate cowboy. Quint had tried to intervene, but was struck from behind just before the shooting began. He had only a brief glimpse of the killer—the man's face bore a dollar-sized birthmark beneath several days' worth of whiskers. The beard over the birthmark showed white. Quint had implored the local law to go after the man, who left town in a hurry. His cries went unheeded. The killing was deemed self-defense, even though the victim's gun never left its holster. Quint had done some investigating of his own—the lateness of the hour and the general intoxication of all the saloon patrons left memories hazy. Quint reluctantly left Abilene when his money ran out.

Sickened by his friend's murder, and burned out on trail drives, Quint wandered into the growing town of Wolf Creek. It was a wide open place—the railroad brought herds up from Texas, which in turn brought an influx of hell raising drovers into town. In turn, the constabulary had to increase in order to handle the bedlam. When Quint learned of an opening for deputy marshal, he cleaned himself up, rundown boots and all, and applied for the job.

Marshal Sam Gardner had warmed to the idea of hiring a man from outside the area. That way, he later explained, there would be no favoritism, or appearance of it, when it was necessary to arrest men from any of the local ranches. The interview had gone well—Gardner seemed to like Quint's demeanor, and though Quint had no previous experience, his knowledge and understanding of drovers would be a definite asset. The marshal explained he could teach the young man what he needed to get started, and the rest he could learn as he went—that was how Gardner had done it. He swore Quint in and gave him a badge.

For Quint, the job served two purposes. First, of course, he was broke and needed the job— he was near the point of having to sell his horse for eating money. Secondly, though, he would be in a perfect position to administer some delayed justice, should the man with the white-patched face show up in Wolf Creek.

Sam Gardner had taken Quint around town to introduce him to the various business owners soon after he had been sworn in that day, six months ago. The first stop had been Dab Henry, mayor of the town and owner of the Lucky Break Saloon. Quint later learned that Henry, who was around fifty and sported a thick black mustache, had grown up poor in the roughest part of Philadelphia. Nowadays Dab Henry comported himself like the businessman and politician he was—but when pushed, the volatile street youth in him came out with a vengeance.

The Lucky Break, as the named implied, was primarily a gambling establishment. It boasted a roulette wheel, three faro tables, two tables each for poker and monte, and a ninth table that was players' choice, including twenty-one. Henry had several dealers on his payroll, as well as a house gambler—Samuel Jones, an enigmatic man with a sophisticated air who had drifted into town not long before Quint. Henry also had half-a-dozen prostitutes on hand, who serviced their customers upstairs.

After the introduction and handshakes, Quint realized there was a strange tension in the air. The mayor and the marshal watched each other like wolves sizing up who should lead the pack.

"How was business last night?" Sam asked.

Mayor Henry looked away and said, somewhat dismissively, "So-so. I'll let you know all about it later. How'd Breedlove do?"

Sam seemed hesitant to answer, but did so as he walked toward the door. "I'll let you know about that later, Dab. We're just on our way over there now."

From there they had gone to the Wolf's Den Saloon, owned by Ira Breedlove. The Wolf's Den was less genteel in its presentation than the Lucky Break—which in its turn was less genteel than the upscale Eldorado that was located right across the street from the marshal's office. Breedlove had more soiled doves than Henry, and they were soiled harder, not to mention a lot more open about plying their trade. His place also featured gambling, but not as extensively—there were five tables and no roulette wheel, although the Wolf's Den also had a house gambler. Breedlove's was a willowy Virginian named Preston Vance, who presented himself as the consummate Southern gentleman but had a cruel streak a mile wide.

Breedlove was one of the "old guard" of Wolf Creek. He had come to the area with his rancher father in the early 1840s, when he was only a boy—more than a decade before there was even a town there. Tobias Breedlove, owner of the T-Bar-T, had sent his son to St. Louis for an education—but the company he fell in with there taught him a lot more than the classics. Ira disappointed his father when he returned to Wolf Creek—with no intention of taking over the ranch, and every intention of taking over the town.

Ira Breedlove was now in his mid-thirties, with prematurely balding brown hair and an unsettling smile. He dressed well—but wore a pistol on one hip and an Arkansas toothpick on the other.

Quint had immediately noted that the atmosphere between Gardner and Breedlove was very similar to that between the marshal and the mayor—very informal and familiar on the surface, almost like old friends, but also very forced and artificial

"We were busy last night, Sam," Breedlove said. "I expect Dab was, too?"

Sam's smile was as cool as the saloon owner's. "I won't know until things are tallied up, later."

It seemed to Quint that competitors Henry and Breedlove kept close tabs on one another, and Sam Gardner was caught in the middle. Or had put himself there. The new deputy was disturbed by the marshal's preoccupation with the saloons' take for the night—he hoped it didn't mean Gardner was taking a percentage, but kept his suspicions to himself.

Things were different at the south end of town, at the end of Second Street. Gardner and Quint stood in the street, with Asa's Saloon on one side and the Red Chamber on the other. The marshal made no move to enter either one. Instead he yelled toward Asa's open door.

"Asa Pepper! Get your wrinkled black ass out here!"

Then he turned toward the opium den. One of Tsu Chiao's nephews was outside, emptying a slop bucket. Sam pointed at him.

"You there. Yes, you. Fetch your uncle out here, I need to talk to him."

The young Chinese man froze in his tracks, obviously confused.

"Oh, for Pete's sake," Sam said, frustrated. "You fetchee honorable goddamned Soo Chow, chop chop, you ignorant Celestial bastard."

The youth nodded his understanding and disappeared inside. From across the street, Asa called out as he approached the lawmen.

"You called for me, suh?"

"Yes I did, and at least you came when I called you.

18

You're an ugly and untrustworthy little son of a bitch, Asa, but at least you're a Christian that speaks English."

"I reckon so, suh."

Tsu Chiao had come outside as well. "Hello, Marshal," he said. Sam did not return the greeting.

"All right," the marshal said. "Now that I've got you both out here, I can make the introductions." He gestured at Quint. "This is Deputy Marshal Quint Croy! What he says goes! If you give him any trouble, I'll be down here like a bolt of lightning hitting the earth."

Asa Pepper nodded. "We always do what you say, Marshal. We respect the law around here."

"Respect the law, my ass," Sam muttered.

"It is not necessary to be rude, Marshal," Tsu Chiao said mildly. "We do not break any laws." Sam glared at him.

Those were the only four establishments that Sam escorted Quint to on that first day on the job. He told the new deputy to introduce and familiarize himself with the rest of Wolf Creek on his own.

"Not much to it, Quint. Walk around and get to know everyone. Keep in mind that anything north of Grant Street is pretty mild compared to what goes on south of there in Dogleg City. Down there will be your territory, on the night shift. You need to rule it with an iron hand and let them know that you won't put up with any horseshit. My other deputy, Fred Garvey—you'll meet him soon enough—has been handling that part of town, but I'm moving him to patrol the north end till things close up, and to be handy in the afternoons."

Quint had been confident about his new responsibilities. The marshal and his deputies in Abilene had been lazy and inattentive—in Wolf Creek, so far as

Quint was concerned, things would be just and fair, with all the evidence gathered before judgment was passed.

Quint got his first real clue as to how things were run in Wolf Creek when he knocked on the door of the building that folks around town jokingly called "Abby Potter's School for Wayward Girls." He'd already heard that it was actually a whore house for upper class clientele. A tiny woman a few years older than Quint, with a ready smile on her face, opened the door. She frowned suddenly when she saw Quint's badge.

"Howdy, ma'am," he said. "My name is Quint Croy. I'm the new deputy marshal."

"I'm Abby Potter—and if you're the new deputy, I guess you know what I do."

"Um, yes, ma'am. Marshal Gardner said I ought to go around town and get acquainted."

"Figures you'd have your hand out like the rest of them," she said. "How do you take yours, deputy—in cash or by a free poke?"

Quint was taken aback. "Oh no, ma'am. I get paid by the marshal's office—no need for anything extra."

Abby's face showed her astonishment, then the smile returned to her face. "Well I haven't heard anything that refreshing in a long time. Quint, I can see that you and I are going to get along fine." She winked. "There might even be an occasional free one in it for you, anyways."

Quint's face flushed, and he muttered, "I just wanted to come by and introduce myself. If you have any trouble, just send someone out to the marshal's office."

Quint had walked away, feeling a little disturbed. It seemed obvious that Abby Potter was making payouts to the marshal, probably in return for working her trade undisturbed. He realized that was probably also what had been going on with the owners of the Lucky Break and the Wolf's Den. Sam's bristly treatment of Asa Pepper and Soo Chow might mean they didn't have such an agreement with him—or maybe it meant that they did, but since they weren't white he didn't feel the need to be deferential toward them. He also realized that, if Sam Gardner were corrupt, the marshal needn't keep it a secret to protect his job—since the mayor was one of the people paying him off.

Several months had gone by since that day, and not much had changed. Sam was spending more and more of his evening hours at the Wolf's Den, the Eldorado, and the Lucky Break, especially since he had been shot in the leg a month or so back—leaving the affairs and patrolling of Wolf Creek and Dogleg City up to his deputies. Deputy Fred Garvey, a middle-aged Georgian who seemed to fit right in with Sam Gardner's amoral approach to peacekeeping, had been killed in the Danby Gang's bank raid, the same occasion on which Sam was wounded. A new man had been hired just a few days ago—a hulking bear of an Irishman named Seamus O'Connor, who had served as a policeman in the infamous Five Points neighborhood of New York City. Quint had already figured out that "experienced policeman," in O'Connor's case, meant he was experienced at taking graft and would also fit right in.

Quint was content with his job and the pay that he received for it. Fifty dollars a month, together with room and meals, was more than he could make herding cattle. Quint didn't attempt to find out the particulars of Sam Gardner's arrangements with the shady business owners of Dogleg City. It seemed that under the table payouts—while not moral—were accepted as a matter of course by all concerned.

And he had to admit, apart from that aspect of the marshal's office, Sam Gardner really had shown himself to be an effective peacekeeper. He kept the rowdies in line, without scaring them and their spending money away from the town altogether. He stood up to bullies and mean drunks with nerves of steel, and was generally fair in his treatment of them. And when that small army of ex-guerrillas had raided the town and robbed the bank, Gardner and Garvey put themselves into the line of fire without a second thought. It cost the Georgia deputy his life, and cost the marshal a bullet in his leg. Quint did not doubt the new deputy, O'Connor, would prove to be just as brave.

But Quint wanted nothing to do with their other activities. He minded his own business in that regard. Quint Croy was a simple man. His job was to keep peace in Dogleg City—and when that peace was broken he did something about it.

* * *

The deputy was shaken from his early morning reverie by the sound of faint footfalls on the outside boardwalk, and a moment later the front door opened. Quint looked up to see the owner of Li Wong's Laundry standing in the doorway. The slight man had a blank, wide eyed expression on his face. Li Wong beckoned to Quint with his right arm. "You come!" he said.

Quint wondered at the Chinese man's action. He knew that Li Wong spoke little English, but was able to understand all that was said to him in that language.

"Do you have a problem, Li Wong?"

The little man motioned again. "You come, De-pu-tee," he insisted. Quint stood and walked toward the

22

door. Li Wong stepped away when Quint neared, motioning with his arm again. Quint trailed behind Li Wong, figuring to follow him to the laundry a block west on South street. Li Wong walked briskly ahead of Quint, cautiously turning his head from time to time to see if the deputy was still following him. Li Wong walked on past his laundry business on Third Street and on to Second Street. He turned left, then crossed over Grant Street into the rough side of town, the neighborhood which the locals called Dogleg City, then kept going.

They walked past the Lucky Break saloon. The place was closed, as it ought to be at this hour. There were no boardwalks in front of the buildings in that part of town, so Quint and Li Wong walked down the middle of the somewhat rutted, dusty street. Quint was very familiar with the businesses down the street at the southernmost end of town, where nightly occurrences of violence were common. The business buildings and the shacks of Cribtown, south of Grant Street, carried an air of impermanence. Constructed of cheap pine lumber, they would have a short lifetime, most likely ending in fire or rot.

At the very end, on the east side, was Asa's saloon—a ramshackle building that housed the lowest class drinking spot in Wolf Creek. The owner and founder, Asa Pepper, had been born a slave sixty years ago. Few locals frequented the place; most of the customers were black cowboys and laborers that arrive with the cattle herds, along with some prairie hide hunters. Mexicans, Indians, and a few whites who did not prefer, or could not afford, the higher side of Wolf Creek's establishments lined up as well. Asa would serve anyone that could put money on the bar. Men came here to escape the hardship of their lives, to guzzle the cheapest whiskey in town, or maybe to spend a little time with a dollar chippy. Women were readily available at Asa's, or—more discreetly—in one of the dozen shacks that were scattered out back, where the women slept after hours.

Quint glanced at the closed door of Asa's as they walked past. It was dark behind the filth-streaked glass. The Red Chamber, an opium den directly across the street, was closed as well. The Red Chamber was owned by Tsu Chiao, another Chinese—everyone pronounced his name "Soo Chow." Quint wondered if Li Wong and Soo Chow had a misunderstanding. Fortunately, Soo Chow spoke English fluently, so maybe they could get to the bottom of this quickly. Li Wong, however, walked on past the Red Chamber. He turned beside Asa's Saloon and headed to the back, toward the whore shacks of Cribtown. As soon as Li Wong reached the back corner of Asa's, he began speaking excitedly in Chinese and pointing.

A man was crumpled on the ground. He lay on his back, open but sightless eyes fixed on the sky. He was dressed in cowboy garb—denim pants, cotton shirt and a cowhide vest. The fly of his pants was open and the end of his pecker, though shriveled, was visible; the whole front of the pants was piss stained. Quint dropped to one knee and touched the back of his hand to the man's neck. It was cold, too cold to have been chilled by the night air alone. He lifted the man's shoulder and looked at his back. He had been shot between the shoulder blades. The heart must have stopped right away as there was not a lot of blood. Quint lowered the body. There was no obvious exit wound. The man had most likely been shot with a pistol, and the ball was lodged somewhere inside. A rifle bullet would have gone clean through.

Quint searched the man's pockets and found $122.00 in bills and a few coins, all of which he stuffed into his own shirt pocket for accounting. He looked for any papers that might indicate who the victim was, but found nothing. The man had a .36 caliber Navy Colt still in its holster. It was fully loaded and unfired. Quint stuck it in his belt. It looked as if the man was most likely taking a leak when someone shot him in the back.

Quint stood and studied the surrounding area, then turned to face Li Wong,

"I suppose you found him while you were making your rounds to pick up some dirty laundry?"

Li Wong nodded. "Miss Haddie say pick up clothes outside early." The Miss Haddie in question, Quint knew, lived and whored in one of the shacks nearby.

Quint knew that Sam would assign him all the investigating leg work, particularly since the killing had taken place in Dogleg City—Quint's unofficially assigned territory. Sam was most likely still in his quarters; the marshal liked to be most visible during the evening gambling hours. It would be up to Quint to notify Elijah Gravely the undertaker to pick up the body, then contact Doctor Munro for his assessment.

Quint pointed toward the street and The Red Chamber. "We could walk over and talk a bit with Soo Chow, see if he has anything to add to this."

Li Wong bristled visibly. Quint knew there was a rift between the two Chinese men—Li Wong disapproved of Tsu Chiao's abusive opium trade at The Red Chamber, and disapproved even more of his unwanted attentions towards Li Wong's sixteen-year-old daughter. Tsu Chiao no doubt figured the nubile young girl would make a prized addition to the wing of his establishment he called "the Jade Chamber."

25

"You can take your cart and go on back to the laundry, Li Wong, I'll speak with Soo Chow later on," Quint said. The relief was evident in Li Wong's face. "You can save me a trip if you would stop by Gravely's Funeral Home and tell Elijah that I need him to come down and pick the body up, I'd appreciate it." Li Wong nodded, then wasted no time in leaving.

Quint turned back to the body to study it for clues. He noticed the man's boots were not new, but were well cared for and recently blacked. The tops of the toes were not worn or scored by stirrups as a drover's boots would be. He picked up one of the man's hands, noting the long slender fingers and the uncallused palms. Despite the man's attire, he was no cowboy.

Quint examined the man's pistol. The Navy Colt had been converted to cartridges from cap and ball. He looked more closely at the finely-tooled, belted holster—the Colt's handle had been facing forward on the left side, available for a convenient draw with the right hand while seated. The man seemed out of place in this cheap part of town—just what was he doing here?

While he waited for Gravely's carriage to show up, Quint walked back between the shacks of Cribtown that sat directly behind Asa's. There was a stench of hastily emptied douche pans and chamber pots about the debris littered place; old clothes, empty bottles, smashed crates and a broken chair were lying about. If the night time revelers ever saw this mess in the light of a sober day, perhaps they would change their mind about ever coming back again.

Quint was looking around, not at anything in particular, when he spotted a pair of legs behind an empty crate. His first thought was that he had discovered another body —but when he walked up, the slight form of Rupe Tingley, the one-armed saloon swamper, began to move. He was just waking up. Quint noticed an empty whisky bottle lying close to the matted grass where the man had been lying.

"What are you doing here, Rupe?"

The man sat up, then rolled around to his knees and stood, using his good arm for support. Rupe looked around through bleary eyes, swaying a little before steadying himself. Quint could smell the foul odor of his whiskey breath. Rupe shook his head a little, as if to clear the cobwebs.

"I don't know, it was dark. I musta fell asleep."

"How long have you been here?"

Rupe shook his head from side to side again. "It was late."

"Did you see or hear anyone shooting behind Asa's last night?"

Rupe dabbed the back of his hand across his reddened eyes. "I can't say," was all he managed before going into a coughing spell.

Quint waited until Rupe had finished gasping for breath, "Are you going to be able to do the cleanup today, Rupe?"

Rupe straightened up a little, pulling his shoulders back. "Damn, sometimes I just cain't drink that stuff like I used to," he said, then coughed again. "I was just heading up to the Lucky Break, Quint."

Rupe stared at Quint as if noticing him for the first time. "Say, deputy, you wouldn't happen to be willing to spot a man an eye opener, would ya?"

Quint reached in his pocket and handed Rupe a nickel; it would cover the price of a beer. Then Quint heard the rumbling of the funeral carriage pulling up behind Asa's to retrieve the body.

Quint wanted to question Rupe further, but not here. He would look him up later when the man was fully functional and take him to the marshal's office. There, just maybe, Rupe might remember something and open up if he got out of his familiar surroundings. At least eliminating the fear of listening ears, which Quint figured were all around this place, might help loosen his tongue.

Quint needed to locate Marshal Sam Gardner and advise him of the killing. He already knew what Sam would most likely say to him, once he heard the news. He would say, "You need to answer the five W's—who, what, where, when and why. When you can answer all of those, you'll have solved the case." Sam had served as captain of an Illinois cavalry company during the war, and had developed a reputation as an efficient lawman in the years since. He was a sharp dresser, and more than a tad vain, but he carried himself with an easy, confident authority. The man had his faults, but he had been very patient in training his young deputy.

* * *

When Quint got to Ma's Café he found Sam at his usual corner table. Ten in the morning was Sam's breakfast hour; he had finished his meal and was sipping coffee. When Quint walked in, Sam knew something was up—he rarely saw his deputy before noon.

Sam swept a hand toward the pot. "Coffee?"

Quint helped himself.

"What have you got, Quint?"

Quint settled into a chair across from Sam. "There was a killing last night, down in Cribtown, right behind

Asa's. The victim was dressed like a working drover but the evidence suggested otherwise."

Quint told of the boots, the soft hands and the money on the man's person.

Sam's eyebrows went up, "Asa's Saloon is the asshole of Wolf Creek. The worst scum frequent that place. A killing anywhere around there is no surprise — but it sounds like your man drifted out of bounds. Any idea as to who he was?"

Quint leaned back in his chair, "I didn't find any papers on him, just $122.00 in bills and change. He had an unfired but fully loaded .36 Colt, still in its holster. It looked to me like the fella didn't want to walk an extra fifty feet to the outhouse, so he stopped in the shadows and was taking a piss when someone shot him in the back. Doc says he figures it happened sometime around midnight."

The marshal's eyebrows went up even further. "Now this is a new wrinkle. While shooting a stranger in Cribtown is not that unusual, not robbing him afterwards is dumbfounding. Hell, it's mildly astonishing the corpse hadn't been robbed of all clothing and dental fillings. Were there any witnesses?"

"I haven't been able to interview anyone from the saloons because all the night people are still sleeping. I did find Rupe Tingley sleeping on the ground behind one of the shacks in Cribtown. He looked to be in pretty rough shape. I figure we ought to talk to him later, when he's fully awake. He may have seen something, but I don't know how we'd get him to talk about it. When I asked him if he saw a shooting, he just said that he couldn't say."

Sam nodded. "Could be that Rupe was seeing elephants last night—but like you say, we'll talk with him later. You've sure enough been busy this morning Quint, but as you know, there's more to do. The objective right now is to find out who the fellow was. You need to go over and let the Sheriff's office know about the killing— see if Sheriff Satterlee has any reward dodgers on the man."

Quint nodded. Sam picked up the coffeepot and waved it in the deputy's direction—Quint declined, so the marshal poured himself another cup. Then he continued his instructions.

"After that you can go on over to the livery, see if there's an unclaimed horse. Check with Richard Wilhite over at the Imperial Hotel—maybe he remembers something about the stranger, and for sure he'll have a signature on the registry. Then you'll need to go down to Dogleg City and grill the hell out of Asa Pepper. I find it hard to believe somebody can get shot outside Asa's place and him know nothing about it. See Soo Chow over at the Red Chamber too, while you're at it. I don't know if it'll do any good going very far into Cribtown—those women that work the area aren't apt to say much even if they know anything. You might talk to Haddie, that whore that lives in the first shack on the left, though, she's always been cooperative."

"All right, Sam," Quint said. "After I go to the Sheriff, the hotel, and see Ben Tolliver at the livery, I'll start off at the high end of town and work on down to the worst places—the way a working cowboy would drink his way through town."

Sam Gardner nodded his approval. "You've got a full plate, then, Quint. I'll help out as much as I can. When we leave here, I'll go by Gravely's and have a look at the corpse, get his description in my mind, the clothes he was wearing and such. I'll let Mayor Henry know over at the Lucky Break, and I was going to see Ira Breedlove at the Wolf's Den anyway so I'll ask around there. This afternoon, when they all wake up, I'll venture into Abby Potter's whore house and see if she or any of the girls knew of the man. Let's meet back here around noon and compare notes."

* * *

Quint took it upon himself to stop in at the Lucky Break, even though Sam had said he was going by the place as well. Quint wanted to do some digging around of his own, and see if he could figure out a motive for the killing.

Rob Parker, the Lucky Break's head bartender, was bleary-eyed—he had not been awake long. The burly, bearded man yawned heavily as he washed glasses.

"Mornin', Rob," Quint said. "Boy, you look like hell this time of day."

Rob shrugged. "You look like hell ever' time of day."

"I can't argue with that. Say, we found a fresh corpse down by Cribtown this morning—I was wondering if you saw him in here at any time last night."

"Ever'body I saw was alive, or close to it. Anything particular I'm supposed to be remembering?"

"This fella was a tall man, in his mid-thirties. Brown hair, pock-marked face—dressed like a drover."

Rob's eyes shifted from his polishing cloth to Quint. "Pock-marked, huh. I do remember seeing a man of that description in here."

"You say you talked to this fella last night?" Quint asked.

"No, I said that I saw a man of that description in here last night. I didn't get a name. He liked to talk, I know that. Seems like he was gabbing to anyone who would listen the whole time he was here–until he came across Alexander Munder, anyways. Munder is immune to other people's voices—he gave Pock-Marks an earful about his cold-hearted wife, until Munder found someone else to glom onto."

Quint nodded; everyone in town knew to avoid Alexander Munder when he was drinking, which was most of the time. He owned a spread a few miles outside town, and had a beautiful wife, but they apparently made each other miserable. When the rancher wasn't drinking he was throwing his money away on whores—it was none of Quint's business, but he suspected that sort of behavior, and the attendant expense, didn't make the man's domestic situation any better.

"Pock tried to shoot the breeze with me, too," the bartender said. "I didn't have time to talk, but I remember getting him a couple beers at the bar—then, later on, he left. It was pretty busy last night, but I think it might have been around midnight. It was late, that's all I know."

"A stranger comes in, has a couple drinks, but he didn't do any gambling, huh?" Quint pried.

Rob Parker worried a cloth in an effort to polish a glass. He paused for a moment, setting the glass down. "I didn't see him gambling—but like I said, we were busy." Rob was getting unsettled by the questions and was becoming evasive, choosing his words carefully.

"What the hell am I supposed to do, Quint, know everything about everybody?"

Quint did not flinch nor turn his gaze from the much larger man, "No, Rob, you don't have to know everything. It's just that I don't see anyone coming in here to have a social drink—if they wanted that, they'd stay up to the Eldorado. People come to the Lucky Break to gamble, pure and simple."

Rob glared at him. Quint pushed a little further.

"That is," he said, "unless he was here on Mister Henry's behalf."

"You'd have to ask Dab about that," Rob was quick to answer.

Dab Henry was in his office, but the door was open—he clearly overheard Quint's questioning his bartender in the almost empty saloon. He walked behind the bar to stand beside Rob Parker, then directed a question to Quint.

"Why all the fuss over a dead drifter?"

Quint raised his eyes to the mayor and said, "If I was a drifter from out of town and caught a bullet, I'd want someone to be curious enough to at least find out my name and why I was shot. Wouldn't you want to know?"

Dab Henry looked at Quint Croy for a studied moment, and spoke softly. "I've seen plenty of drifters come to town with the thought they was going to beat the house gamblers and walk away flush. Most of them leave broke. Hell, the man was most likely a criminal anyway, and was running from something in his past. Somebody caught up to him and finished the job. That's how I see it."

Quint smiled politely, but his eyes darkened. "That may be true, but a man's dead and I aim to find out who he was and why somebody killed him."

Dab watched Quint until he had disappeared out the door. Then he went to his office for his coat and hat.

* * *

When Sam Gardner entered the marshal's office a half-hour before noon, Dab Henry stepped in right behind him. Sam slid into the chair behind his desk. Dab, his face flushed from the walk, took a chair beside him. He got right to the point of the visit.

"That baby faced deputy you got is poking his nose a little too deeply into things that are not of public record."

Sam was unmoved, indicating so with his flat reply. "Quint is investigating a murder."

"That, I am painfully aware of," Dab said sourly. "He came into the Lucky Break, grilled Rob Parker and made insinuations that the dead man might be working for me. That's ludicrous! From the description, I didn't know the man. I never laid eyes on him. I wouldn't be a bit surprised if Ira Breedlove isn't behind this—trying to put me and the Lucky Break in a bad light, making folks afraid to go there, so that he can get a bigger cut of the town business."

Sam looked at Dab for a moment. "The Wolf's Den sells more whiskey than the Lucky Break, but you get more of the gambling. The whores at both places charge about the same. So I don't see where either place is getting one up on the other."

"If it was up to Breedlove, I'd be out of business!" Dab said sourly.

When Sam didn't reply, Dab said, "I think it would be wise if you put a leash on your boy Quint before he causes some real problems."

Sam sat silently for a moment, allowing the intended effect of Dab's remarks to soften. "Somebody got killed in his territory on his watch, and he needs to investigate. It's what he gets paid to do."

Dab leaned forward.

"Sam," Dab said with a low-toned seriousness, "men like you are necessary for the safety of our citizens. Someone that's strong with authority, for the folks to look up to and call on when there is trouble. That doesn't make you a creator, though. It takes someone like me, with a certain ruthlessness, to be a creator, to see things through, even if it means stepping on a few toes. People respect you and your office. Me, I never gave a tinker's damn what some of these low life folks think of me. I've pushed a few around, when they got out of line, because they are not creators. If I hadn't done it, then others would have. Everyone depends on me to come through, because I create jobs and wealth. You yourself are one of the beneficiaries of that creation—on a regular and unofficial basis."

Sam sat silently, waiting for Dab to finish his rant. He had never particularly liked Dab personally, and didn't care for the mayor reminding him of the extra payment that had been arranged between them. He would not allow Dab's snide reminders or harsh words, however, to influence the job he was to do.

"Most folks figure that those in charge of the gambling and the running of a few whores are expected to be a little one-sided in favor of the house," Sam said. "But murder is different—otherwise, folks would just do as their mood dictated. Some of your gaming tables are a bit tilted, and so are Ira Breedlove's—to the benefit of us all—but that doesn't entitle anyone to buy this badge."

Dab's face flushed a little, but he did not have a ready reply.

Sam stood up. "Dab, I've got to get back on the street and give Quint a hand in this. Besides, I expect you have a sight of creating to do this afternoon, and I hate to hold you back from it."

Dab stood and put his hat on. "Would you at least speak to Quint, and have him ease off just a bit?"

Sam nodded as he escorted Dab to the door. Once the mayor was out of sight, the marshal limped back to his desk and sat down again.

* * *

After Quint left the Lucky Break, he figured it was time to talk to Asa Pepper. Quint got along well with Asa, despite Sam's attitude and rough treatment of the man. Quint had chosen a more genial approach to Asa after Sam's rude introduction. He had returned to the saloon shortly afterward and engaged Asa in a long conversation, resulting in the two shaking hands and vowing to get along together fairly.

One evening, two weeks after the deputy had first met the black saloonkeeper, while on a routine patrol, Quint walked into the saloon to see a drunken black cowboy waving an eight-inch knife in Asa's face. The cowboy had Asa backed up to a wall, and said, "I'll cut your guts out!" Quint didn't waste any time—he rushed close and whacked the cowboy over the head with the butt of his pistol, then dragged him off to jail. Since that incident, Quint and Asa's relationship had grown into a respectful alliance between the two men. Quint visited Asa daily and the two would talk about the troubles of the night before—and occasionally of fishing, which both men held an affinity for.

Inside the dank interior of Asa's, two cowboys sat at a table and a tall swarthy Mexican vaquero with a drooping mustache was standing at the far end of the bar talking to a skinny woman dressed in a flimsy red dress. The vaquero was wearing a long barreled six-gun, the nose of the holster strapped to his leg. When he saw the badge on Quint's shirt, he moved his hand close to the butt of his six-gun and offered a stern faced, squinty-eyed stare. Quint was used to such behavior by the patrons of Dogleg City. A good many were on the dodge. Quint paid the man no mind, and walked up to face Asa Pepper.

"Mornin', deputy," Asa offered.

Quint spent the next few minutes telling Asa about the body behind the saloon, giving the dead man's description.

"Was there a ruckus in here last night, Asa?"

"They's a ruckus in here most every night, Quint, you know that," Asa said.

"Do you remember if the man I described was in here?"

"Yeah, I remember the pock-faced man. He's been in two nights in a row. Comes in late, has a beer or so, then leaves. I don't know where he come from or where he goes."

"Was there anything unusual about him?" Quint asked.

"Jes' his mouth. He say he'd like to put me on the right track. Send more business my way. I think he works for Ira Breedlove."

"Why do you say that?"

"Ira loaned me some money, a while back, when the saloon was having a tough time. Sometimes I've been a little late making my payments. When this fella comes in, all he talks about is paying a little money. So I figure he's working for Breedlove."

"Did he ever say so?" Quint asked.

"No, he kept saying a little now will get me a lot later. I ain't sorry that the man is gone, but I don't know anything about who went and shot him."

When Quint walked into the marshal's office at five minutes to noon, Sam Gardner was seated at his desk. "What did you get for me, Quint?"

Quint started talking before he sat down.

"The man's name is Laird Jenkins, according to the Imperial's register. I don't believe he was just a drifter—there were no saddle bags and no horse at the livery. According to Clay Willard the stationmaster, the said Jenkins came in on the westbound train three days ago from St. Louis. I looked through his room at the Imperial—I found only a change of work clothes, and a set of fancier traveling clothes in a carpetbag. He must have been planning on staying a while, because I didn't locate a return ticket or any kind of papers. He spent his afternoons gambling at the Eldorado, then evenings at The Lucky Break, and lastly Asa's. I haven't talked to anyone at the Wolf's Den, but I assume that he stopped in there, too. He took his meals at Isabella's restaurant. Everybody has seen him but nobody knows him. Except whoever he was working for, of course."

"You believe he was working for someone?" Sam asked.

"When I asked Asa Pepper who he thought the fella was, he said that he thinks he might work for Ira Breedlove. Asa said that he owes Breedlove some money, and maybe Breedlove sent the guy to pressure him."

Sam raised his eyebrows, "That could be so. I believe that Ira Breedlove is almost as grubbing as Dab Henry, when it comes to money."

"I think it goes a little deeper than that," Quint replied. "Asa said he didn't know of, or have anything to do with, the shooting—and I believe him. And it wouldn't make any sense for Breedlove to kill off his own man, if that's what Laird was. So I figure it was maybe a random killing, perhaps a mistaken identity, or else someone sending a message to Ira Breedlove."

"You say you haven't been to the Wolf's Den?" Sam asked.

"No, you said you were going there," Quint said.

"I did, but Ira wasn't there. I did go to The Lucky Break, but that was before you went there, too." Sam sounded annoyed.

"I thought it was important to talk to Rob Parker, to see if he remembered the man," Quint said quietly.

Sam nodded, "Dab Henry showed up here to complain about your questioning. Dab can be scornful at times—it might be best if I handle him and Ira Breedlove."

Quint was happy to let him. The deputy intended to go to his room at Rose Cotton's boarding house and hit the mattress. The only good thing about staying up this long past his bedtime was that he would be too tired to dream he was still making his rounds in Dogleg City.

CHAPTER TWO

Samuel Jones sat at his usual table in the Lucky Break. It damn well better be his table, because he paid Dab Henry a thousand a month for the right to deal his cards there. Not yet noon, and Samuel dealt himself a hand of solitaire. Sometimes he couldn't even beat himself, but he never cheated. Lots of gentlemen did. Three-card monte players did. Faro dealers did. But Samuel Jones didn't, and everyone in Dogleg City knew it. He started lining up the cards.

A teamster pushed his way into the Lucky Break and hollered. "Hey Mister Henry. Yer mirror's here."

Dab burst from the back room—he had only been back from his visit at the marshal's office for a few minutes. "You all be careful with that glass," he hollered back. "Cost a pretty piece, but it'll put the Lucky Break up a notch or two. People're gonna flock right in here to look at themselves in that big ol' thing."

The mirror sat tied to an A-frame on a wagon. Little bags stuffed with raw cotton cushioned it against bumps in the road. Four teamsters lifted it from the frame as if it were pure crystal and would shatter if they breathed on it wrong.

Samuel Jones grinned at the antics and dealt himself another card. Karl Shultz, the cabinet maker from Joseph

Nash's carpentry shop, squeezed in as the teamsters manhandled the mirror in. He rubbed his hands together in glee. "I've already made the upper framework," he said to the teamsters. "Just slide the top of the mirror into the groove up there. Careful now. Don't push too hard. Okay. Slide the bottom of the mirror into place. Yes. Exactly right. Now, let me fix it in there with these wedges." He showed a handful of oak wedges about two inches wide and only as thick as a fingernail at one edge and nearly a quarter of an inch at the other end. Slipping a wedge between the cabinet and the mirror's bottom edge every foot or so, he used a little rawhide mallet to tap the wedges home, and the mirror stood straight and firm at back of the Lucky Break bar. Karl affixed a carved molding at the bottom to conceal the wedges and make the mirror look precisely mounted.

"There," Karl said. "Mister Henry, you have the finest bar mirror in Dogleg City, if not all of Wolf Creek."

Dab echoed Karl's words. "There you have it, only at the Lucky Break."

Samuel Jones smiled slightly at the pride in Henry's voice. He glanced at the mirror and then back to his game. Then the image in the mirror registered.

Valentine Hébert.

The gambler looked back at the mirror, but the New Orleans dandy was gone. Samuel quickly scanned the Lucky Break. No one he could see resembled Valentine Hébert. A mistake? He looked around again, making sure he saw every person in the room. No Hébert. Still, Samuel Jones trusted his own eyesight. Too many times it had proved correct, and because of that, he was still alive. Thrice up and down the Santa Fe Trail with Hank

Brockman's wagon trains of big Murphys. Countless times up and down Ol' Miss aboard the *Delta Princess*. The last Delacorte man had tried to kill Samuel Jones on the *Princess*. Samuel still bore the scar the bullet sliced across his face just below his cheekbone. The Delacorte man took a round in the breastbone from Samuel's pocket Colt and toppled into the frothy water churned by the stern wheel. That's when Samuel decided to make his living on dry land.

Hébert.

Samuel remembered well the last time he'd seen Hébert. Spring in New Orleans, 1855.

* * *

Back then Samuel Jones had been known as Philippe Beaumont, and made his living as an assassin.

Sometimes he went a month without killing, never two. On April 14, 1855, Beaumont stood beneath the dueling oaks of City Park in New Orleans. He'd been forced to choose dawn because others had already set more reasonable hours at which to defend their honor. The approaching morning grayed the spaces between the giant live oaks. Tendrils of night fog seemed to drag at the tree trunks with wraithly fingers as they surrendered to the day. Beaumont's horse snorted.

"Monsieur Larouche's party arrives, sir," said Marcel, Beaumont's quadroon manservant.

Beaumont nodded. He hoped his second, Claude Bucher, would not impinge upon his honor by being unconscionably late. He stepped from under the oak to greet his opponent. His sudden movement startled the doves roosting in the branches and made them stir about and chortle among themselves. Ha, symbol of peace, he thought—more men have died on this dueling field than fell to British bullets in the Battle of New Orleans.

"*Bonjour, mes amis.* The mists have lifted, Monsieur Larouche. It seems a fine morning in which to defend one's honor, no?" Beaumont doffed his silk top hat and bowed to the Larouche entourage.

"God damn your honor, Beaumont. Where is your second? Let's get on with it."

Beaumont noticed a slight quaver in young Larouche's voice, and his hands shook as he removed his gloves. A sense of calm settled over Beaumont. He remembered the challenge.

Three days earlier, a packet had arrived at Beaumont's residence containing a demand draft for five hundred dollars on the Bank of Orleans and a note: ANNALISA MUST NOT CONSORT WITH LAROUCHE. SEE TO IT.

Beaumont learned that Larouche was to attend a soirée on Chartres Street the following evening, and used his connections to obtain an invitation as well. Beaumont entered the party with Elizabeth, an octoroon, on his arm. With his usual dexterity of arrangements, he seated his lady friend in the chair next to Annalisa Delacorte, whom Larouche accompanied. He and Elizabeth did not dance. Theirs was another mission.

Larouche escorted Annalisa back from the dance floor and repositioned her chair. While seating her, he moved it imperceptibly closer to Elizabeth. Immediately Beaumont was at Larouche's side. He spoke too low for anyone but Larouche to hear. "Your presence on the balcony, monsieur," he said, and left the hall.

"What's this all about, Beaumont?" Larouche said as he came through the doors to the balcony.

Beaumont stepped forward and slapped Delacorte in the face with his gloves. "You, monsieur, crowded my lady and I would satisfy my honor."

Anger blazed in Larouche's eyes. "As you wish, monsieur."

"Name your second. Mine will call upon him." Beaumont strode away, his frock coat billowing behind his knees. The seconds had set Sunday for the duel. Larouche knew he was no match for Beaumont with swords, so he chose pistols at twenty paces. The challenged party provided the weapons.

"Ah, my second arrives," said Beaumont. He nodded toward his associate Jean Bucher's slight form hurrying through the dew-drenched grass.

The duelists gathered beneath the tree. Larouche's weapon bearer opened an elaborately carved box to reveal two perfectly matched Belgian flintlock dueling pistols in the Henry Lapage style. Beaumont glanced at Larouche. A sheen of perspiration coated the young man's face. Beaumont took both pistols from their pockets in the case. His superb sense of balance told him the pistols were true matches, neither with an advantage over the other. He reversed them, grasped the pistols by the trigger guard, and offered them butt-first to Larouche.

"*Choisez, mon ami,*" he said.

Larouche's trembling hand reached for the left, then the right. He searched Beaumont's face with tortured eyes.

"I relinquish my right of first choice to you, monsieur. Please." Beaumont thrust the two dueling pistols at his adversary.

Larouche peered at the left hand pistol, then the right hand one. A rivulet of perspiration trickled from beneath his sideburn. He took a deep breath and grasped the pistol Beaumont held in his left hand. "This one," he said.

"It is a fine pistol," Beaumont said. "You made an excellent choice."

From the branches of the oak tree above their heads came a warm, wet missile, which splatted on Beaumont's hand and splattered across the scrollwork of the dueling pistol. "*Merde*," Beaumont said. *This is a shitty business, he thought.* And suddenly he wished he didn't have to kill the young man who stood sweating and trembling with a Belgian dueling pistol in his hand. "Mark off twenty paces," he said as he cleaned the dove droppings from his hand.

Marcel measured the field of fire. Larouche's second checked his measurements. The distance was correct. "Pick your position, monsieur," Jean Bucher said— etiquette dictated that the challenger's second count the duel.

Larouche bowed his head. Perhaps he was praying. He took a deep breath and marched to the northern marker. He stood facing north.

Beaumont went to the south marker and faced south.

"At the count of five, you will turn and shoot," Jean Bucher said. "If both parties are still standing after both weapons have been fired, they will be reloaded and you will shoot again. Cock your weapons."

The double click of cocking hammers rang loud in the gray dawn light.

"Ready your weapons."

The duelists brought their pistols to their shoulders, muzzles skyward.

Jean Bucher counted. "One."

"Two."

"Three."

"Four."

"Five."

Both men turned sideways to their opponent.

Larouche fired. The .58 caliber ball smashed into Beaumont's open double-breasted frock coat just behind its first button, plowed a furrow in the skin over his sternum and exited through the lefthand button.

The recoil of the dueling pistol lifted Larouche's right arm high.

Beaumont lifted his own pistol, adjusted it higher, and fired.

His ball hit exactly where he aimed, at a wood dove on a limb above Larouche. The heavy ball smashed the small bird to bits, and its blood splattered Larouche's hair and clothing.

Beaumont lowered his pistol with a smile on his face. "Ah, I see that I have brought blood. That is blood on your tunic, is it not?" He waved toward Larouche, who wiped at the gore that now marred his impeccable attire.

The dueling pistol held at his side, Beaumont strode to Larouche's position. "As I drew blood, monsieur, I declare my honor satisfied. Does that meet with your approval?"

Young Larouche sputtered. Then it dawned upon him what Beaumont was doing. He no longer had to stand beneath the dueling oaks until either he or Beaumont was dead. "Satisfied? But of course, I agree."

For a moment, Larouche's second stood motionless. Then he strode across the grass to stand by his man. "*Mes amis*, Monsieur Larouche has fulfilled his obligation to Monsieur Beaumont," he said.

Beaumont reversed the dueling pistol and held it out to Larouche butt first. The second took the gun.

From the inner pocket of his frock coat, Beaumont withdrew a bank draft for five hundred dollars. It was signed by T. Delacorte. He handed it to Larouche, who read it, then looked at Beaumont with a question on his face.

"That is how much your life is worth, young Larouche," Beaumont said. "I'd advise you to stay away from Annalisa. I'm not the only person in New Orleans who might call you out for the right price."

Clouds covered the face of Larouche's second. He was a Delacorte man, and therefore wanted Larouche dead. But now he was forced to announce Beaumont's honor satisfied. His name was Valentine Hébert.

* * *

Philippe Beaumont disappeared after his duel with Andre Larouche, and though he searched and searched, Hébert had not been able to find the assassin. His frustration grew as the years seemed to float away.

Hébert spent a few years fighting Yankees along the Mississippi, but since then, he'd searched for Philippe Beaumont, his expenses borne by the family Delacorte. The old man who'd paid for the assassination of Andre Larouche barely hung onto life, but his sons and daughter still wanted satisfaction, and that satisfaction could only be gained with the death of the man who had shamed the family by exposing their willingness to hire the death of Annalisa's suitor. Young Larouche disappeared as well, but no one thought him of enough consequence to look for.

Delacorte's agent Louis Sarazin sent word a few months ago that Philippe Beaumont lived on the Delta Princess, and was now a professional gambler who used the name Samuel Jones. Then Sarazin disappeared. He booked passage on the *Delta Princess* from St. Louis, but never arrived in New Orleans.

"The assassin was on the *Delta Princess*," Marcel Delacorte had said, hissing in his anger. "*There*. Sarazin *said* he was there. But now even Sarazin is gone, disappeared."

He turned on Hébert, spraying him with saliva as he shouted. "Find that man. I. Want. Him. Dead. *Comprenez-vous?*"

"*Je comprends parfaitetment*," Hébert had replied. "I understand perfectly."

Hébert booked passage on the *Delta Princess* himself. By the time the *Princess* docked at Laclede's Landing in St. Louis, Hébert knew Samuel Jones had not been seen aboard the riverboat after it landed there two trips before. No one knew of a passenger named Louis Sarazin. But then, no crew of a boat that catered to wealthy patrons and prime cotton would admit that a passenger had disappeared.

Hébert, too, left the *Delta Princess* in St. Louis. When a man's on the run, he naturally heads west. No one asks questions on the frontier. Too many men and not a few women have secrets they'd rather not have bared. Following his instinct, Hébert took a steamer to Kansas City.

Samuel Jones was a professional gambler, albeit an honest one. Herds of longhorns came up from Texas along the Chisholm Trail. That meant cowboys with money to spend, businessmen with money to buy beeves, drummers and saloons and general stores and emporiums and opium dens and dirty dove joints. Hébert checked the towns at trails end. Trains at Wolf Creek, not far north of the Indian Nations, loaded nearly a hundred thousand head of cattle bound for Chicago in 1870. To Hébert, that many steers meant a pool of money that no professional gambler could resist. Not as easy as the Mississippi, of course, but undoubtedly lucrative.

Delacorte's man Hébert stepped off the Atchison, Topeka & Santa Fe train at the railhead in Wolf Creek. He checked into the Imperial Hotel, an imposing structure for a town that had sprung from nothing but a few shacks in the curve of Wolf Creek before the cattle had come. The room was more than comfortable, too. As soon as he deposited his carpetbag in the room, he went back down to the lobby.

The front desk clerk was all attention as Hébert approached. "May I be of service, sir?" he said.

"If a man were to wish to game a bit," Hébert said, "where would he go in this town?"

"Game?"

"Why games of chance, of course. Roulette, for instance. Or monte."

"Ah, gambling. Yes, sir. Well, you may wish to try the Eldorado on South Street. Further down toward the creek, there's the Wolf Den and the Lucky Break, but they're awful close to Dogleg City."

"Dogleg City? There's another town close by, then?"

"Oh no, sir. Across Ulysses S. Grant Street, all the way to Wolf Creek itself, is what we call Dogleg City. One who treasures his life would not venture across Useless Grant Street. Er, that's what the cowboys call it, anyway."

"Thank you. Now, where do I look for the sheriff or marshal or whomever passes for keepers of the law in this city?"

"The marshal of Wolf Creek is Sam Gardner, and his office is on Fourth and South Street." The clerk waved in the general direction of the office. "Over that way. You can't miss it."

"Thank you. I'll wander over to see him, then." Hébert started to leave, then turned to ask one more question. "Which of these—Dogleg City—establishments is closest?"

"That'd be the Lucky Break, Mister. If you just head down Second Street here you'll run smack into it."

Hébert nodded and left the hotel. He followed the clerk's directions and headed for the Lucky Break. He stuck his head inside briefly; workmen were installing a new mirror, and the owner was directing the activity. Hébert heard someone address the owner as "mayor"—he decided to come back later, after he had checked with the constabulary. He made his way back to South Street and headed east toward the marshal's office.

The marshal's office stood on the corner—the lots on either side were empty. Wolf Creek might be a growing town, but it hadn't grown enough to build boardwalks past vacant lots; they ended abruptly at the corner. The building itself had porches that ran around it, one fronting South Street, one fronting Fourth. The entrance was at the corner of the building. From the street, Hébert could see a wiry man with long black hair bent over a desk, laboriously writing a document.

Hébert mounted the three steps to the porch and tapped on the glass of the door. The black-haired man's right hand went to the ivory handle of a Remington .44. He looked up as Hébert opened the door and walked in.

"Good morning, Marshal. My name is Valentine Hébert. I come from New Orleans, where I am employed by the Delacorte family. Perhaps you have heard of them."

"Sam Gardner," the long-haired man said. He stood and beckoned Hébert to a chair. "How can I help you, Mister Hébert?"

"Actually, I'm searching for a miscreant."

"If you're looking for Miss Creeant, you'd better hoof it over to Miss Abby's on Grant Street." Marshal Gardner's face showed hard lines, and Hébert could not tell if his comment was meant as a joke. If it were, the marshal had a very dry sense of humor.

"Unfortunately, sir, the person is not a woman, but a man. A gambler. A professional, I am told. His name, sir, is Philippe Beaumont. And he is a killer. I also hear that he goes by the name of Samuel Jones."

The corners of Gardner's eyes tightened. He knew Samuel Jones. Hébert had no doubt.

"If you'll just tell me where Jones is, Marshal, I'll leave."

"Sorry, Hébert. Can't say as I recall any gamblers in this town named Jones. But that is an awful common name. Didn't recognize the other one—what did you say, Beaumont?"

Hébert nodded. "You don't mind if I look around?"

"Free country," Gardner said. "But if you shoot one of Wolf Creek's citizens in the back, I'll sure as Hell string you up, if I don't plug you first. You have my word on it."

Hébert gave the marshal a cold smile. "I am somewhat disappointed that you would think a man of my standing would stoop to shooting a man in the back."

51

"Mister, I don't know what you were back in the Louisiana swamp, but here you're just one more jasper I have to keep an eye on. And I'll do just that." The marshal was still in a bad mood from his chat with Dab Henry.

"Very well, I will just have to investigate for myself."

"You do that. Good day." Marshal Gardner sat back down in his chair and returned to his paperwork. He didn't look up when Hébert left. But when his new deputy, Seamus O'Connor came to start his rounds, Gardner said, "O'Conner, you hike over to the Lucky Break and tell Samuel Jones that there's a dude here from New Orleans who calls himself Hay Bear, and that said dude is looking for him."

"Hay Bear? Some kinda Injun?"

"Hell, I don't know. Frenchie, maybe." The marshal grinned to himself.

O'Connor got a sawed-off coach gun from the rack and dropped a handful of shells in his pocket. "Sure and I'll amble on over, boss."

* * *

Valentine Hébert left the marshal's office and went to the Eldorado Saloon, directly across the street. He had no success there—employees and patrons alike developed lockjaw when he described his quarry to them. He then made his way to the Wolf's Den, where he received the same response. He could not help noticing, however, that the establishment's owner—who had introduced himself as Ira Breedlove—watched Hébert's efforts with a wry smile and a keen eye.

"Sorry you didn't find your man here," Breedlove said. "But I do wish you success. I do indeed."

"I'll find him," Hébert said. "The only place I haven't asked for him is the Lucky Break—that has to be where he is."

"It may well be," Breedlove agreed. "They're a sordid bunch over there."

* * *

The Lucky Break's free lunch always attracted a crowd. Today's fare was a deep pot of pork and beans, a mound of saleratus biscuits, a tureen of thick gravy, and a barrel of pickles. Head bartender Rob Parker was directing the activities.

Hal, the daytime bartender, wandered over to the house gambler's table. "You want something to eat, Sam?" he asked.

Samuel shook his head. His mind was still on Hébert, though the dandy had yet to show his face again. Perhaps he'd seen Samuel in the mirror as the gambler had seen him. He checked the Derringer in his sleeve. If he straightened his arm just right, the little gun sprang into his hand already cocked. All he had to do was pull the trigger.

Free lunch eaters were mostly beer drinkers, so the rumble inside the Lucky Break was nothing like the nighttime roar. Still, Samuel didn't hear Deputy O'Connor come through the front door—but as he was glancing into the new mirror regularly, he caught sight of the deputy when he was two steps into the saloon.

O'Connor walked straight to Samuel's table. "Marshal Gardner told me to tell you that some southern dude that calls himself Hay Bear is looking for you. I reckon you Sams must look out for each other."

"You mean Hébert?"

"That's what I said. Hay Bear."

"I saw him," Samuel said. "But he's disappeared. However, he will return sooner or later. He wants to kill me, I suppose."

The deputy's brow furrowed at the latter remark. He opened his mouth to say something, then closed it, probably figuring plenty of people might have reason to kill a professional gambler. "Watch yerself, boyo," O'Connor said then, and walked from the Lucky Break, the sawed-off coach gun in the crook of his arm.

The free lunch crowd left. No one came to Samuel's table. Hardcore gamblers would show up as the day wore on. They always did. He played solitaire. It helped to keep handling the cards, even if no one was at the table. The roulette wheel clicked. The faro dealer's box flapped out its cards. Samuel dealt himself another card.

"Hey, Samuel! What's the chance of me and Howie getting a game going?"

Samuel recognized Billy Below's high-pitched voice. "Welcome gentlemen," he said without looking up. "Have a seat." He then glanced at Billy and his cohort Howie. Cowboys to the core. Not enough pocket money to play more than penny ante poker.

The two cowboys sat down, shit-eating grins on their faces. "Today's my lucky day," Billy said. "I feel it in my bones."

"One's bones are often wrong," Samuel said, matching their grins. How could a man not smile with such good-natured cowboys wanting to play his game?

For an instant, his eyes went from Billy's smiling face to the mirror behind the bar. There stood Valentine Hébert.

Hébert wore a tiny smile on his face, and he carried a wooden case beneath his arm. He nodded a bow in Samuel's direction, and started across the saloon toward Samuel's table.

"Billy. Howie. You'd better stand up and get away. Do me a favor and move over by the bar until this is over, will you?"

"Wha—"

"Move!" Samuel's order cut the air, and Billy and Howie scraped their chairs back and scrambled over to the bar. Samuel stood and turned to meet Hébert, his sword-cane leaning against the table within easy reach.

Hébert stopped two paces from the table. "*Bonjour, Monsieur* Beaumont. Or, should I say, Mister Jones?"

"Valentine." Samuel's hands hung naturally by his sides.

"I came to challenge you, Beaumont, Jones, or whoever you are." Hébert stepped closer and put the wooden box on the table. "The pistols you and Andre Larouche used at City Park."

He opened the box. The Belgian pistols looked burnished and well cared-for. "Take your pick," he said. "Twenty paces at sundown."

"Why wait," Samuel said. "Billy," he called.

"Yeah, Sam."

"Run over to the smithy and ask Angus to come over here, please."

Billy Below read the serious expression on Samuel's face, left his beer on the bar, and sped from the Lucky Break on the run.

"Please take a seat, Valentine. We should do this correctly." Samuel took his seat.

Hébert sat in the chair opposite Samuel. Neither man spoke.

Billy Below came pounding back. "Angus'll be here'n a jif," he said.

"Thank you, Billy." Samuel raised his voice. "Hal, give Billy and Howie another beer on me."

Angus Sweeney strode in, his butternut kepi low over his eyes. He scanned the room, fastened his gaze on Samuel, and walked to the table. "What do you need, Samuel?"

"Angus, this is Valentine Hébert from New Orleans. He has challenged me. Pistols—" he pointed at the Belgian dueling flintlocks "–at twenty paces. You're a southern gentleman and a son of the Crescent City, Angus. Would you please measure the twenty paces and count down for us?"

Sweeney nodded. "I can do that fer y'all. Where?"

"Over on the far side of the livery corral on North Street," Samuel said. "Pace it off north and south so no one is bothered by the sun. Oh, and make sure it's outside the town limits. No need to get Sam Gardner involved. "

"Okay. Give me a few minutes." Sweeney rushed out.

"I assume the pistols are loaded and primed."

"They are," Hébert said.

"Then let us repair to the field of honor," Samuel said. He stood, flicked his Derringer from its clip and laid it on the table. "After you, Valentine," he said.

The two men, so alike in bearing and mien, walked out of the Lucky Break. Hébert carried the box of dueling pistols under his arm. The Lucky Break's patrons mumbled to each other. People began to follow them. The crowd grew. The two men paid no attention, nor did they converse with each other. They merely walked up

Second Street, turned left on North, and went past the livery stable and the corrals. At least fifty people followed, whispering, making bets, ogling Samuel and Hébert.

Sweeney had trampled down the tall grass beyond the Wolf Creek sign, making a fairly straight line running north and south. "How's that, Samuel?"

"Fine. Would you like north or south, Valentine?"

"Let's flip a coin."

Samuel dug a silver dollar from a vest pocket. "Heads or tails?"

"Tails," Hébert said.

Samuel flipped the coin and let it fall on the ground. It landed tails up. "Your choice of weapon or position, Valentine. Which do you prefer?" He picked up the coin.

The crowd lined both sides of the dueling ground. Neither Hébert nor Samuel paid them any attention. "I choose the southerly position, as I am a man of the south," Hébert said.

"Very well. The pistols. Give the box to Angus, if you please."

Hébert handed the box to Sweeney. He opened the box and held it out toward Samuel, who casually chose a pistol. He checked the load and the priming. He inspected the flint and the frizzen. All was in excellent order.

"Gentlemen," Sweeney said in a loud voice. "This is a field of honor. Mister Hébert, will you take the southern position please, facing south. Mister Jones, take the northern position please, facing north."

The duelists took their places.

"At the count of five, you will turn and shoot," Sweeney said. "If both parties are still standing after the weapons have been fired, they will be reloaded and you will shoot again. Cock your weapons."

The hammers cocked with a double click.

"Ready your weapons."

Samuel and Hébert brought their pistols to their shoulders, muzzles skyward.

Sweeney counted. "One."

"Two."

"Three."

"Four."

"Five."

Samuel and Hébert pivoted, presenting their right sides to their opponents. Samuel's face was placid, as if he cared not whether he lived or died, but Hébert's neck above his collar had turned red, and the blood climbed to flush his face. "*Merde*," he shouted, and pulled the trigger.

Samuel Jones stood perfectly still. The .58 caliber ball from Hébert's pistol flew past his head, close enough to ruffle his longish hair.

The recoil of the dueling pistol lifted Hébert's right arm high as Samuel fired. His ball took Hébert beneath his right arm and smashed a rib. The bone deformed the soft lead ball, which tumbled through Hébert's chest cavity, tearing heart and lungs. He dropped to his knees, released the pistol, and fell on his face in the grass.

Sweeney rushed to the fallen man. In a moment, he stood and turned to face Samuel Jones. "We can call Doc Munro if you want, Samuel, but this man's dead."

Samuel Jones carefully placed the dueling pistol in its box and stood for a moment looking at Valentine Hébert's lifeless form. Then, without speaking, he walked back to the Lucky Break. Deputy O'Connor was approaching the crowd, but Samuel did not slow down until he reached the saloon.

"Hal," he said. "Could I have a beer, please?" He sat down at his table and picked up his cards.

CHAPTER THREE

Marshal Sam Gardner massaged his stiff leg and sighed.

"Well, there's no getting around it, old hoss," he said—partly to the appendage and partly to himself, although he supposed it really amounted to the same thing. "Doc Munro said I needed to be exercising you more. We have enough to occupy us for the rest of the day and into the evening, and it looks like we're in for a hike all over Wolf Creek."

Deputy Quint Croy had left the marshal's office, after delivering his report, to finally turn in for the day so he could be fresh for his night shift duties—so there was no one around to hear Sam talking to his own leg. Witnesses might have thought he had already started on the day's ration of whiskey—and, by his own reckoning, that auspicious moment was not far off—but no, it was just Samuel Horace Gardner and his bum limb. He had to admit, it was more of a conversationalist—and certainly listened better—than a good deal of the people he had to deal with in this town.

He stretched back in his chair, reaching into the corner, behind the coat-rack. He pulled out his new walking stick. It was made of fine mahogany, expertly crafted—and at the head, the best part of all. It was carved into the shape of a wolf. The bottom was capped with heavy steel, to protect it from wear as he tapped his way along the boardwalks, and, more importantly, to give it sufficient heft when he swung it through the air and used it to crack the skull of some ne'er-do-well or other. As he was certain he would, and probably before the week was out. He might even have the opportunity to whack a miscreant or two—he smiled again at his little joke to the annoying Frenchie a couple of hours earlier, and of how he had used the pretense of not knowing how to pronounce the man's name as a way to take him down a peg in the eyes of Seamus. He wished he had thought to make the same joke to Hébert, and ruffle his feathers a bit more. The marshal hated being taken for an idiot.

He held it in his hands, once more admiring the workmanship and feeling the balance of it. The marshal had commissioned this fine tool soon after he had been shot by the Danby Gang, from Joseph Nash—the carpenter whose shop was near Doctor Munro's. The man was a virtual magician with saw and lathe. Nash was very unprepossessing, and seemed to be interested only in the items he crafted in his shop, but he had a secret—one which he divulged to Sam some months ago, no doubt because he respected the marshal's wartime reputation.

Joseph Nash, the quiet, shy carpenter, had been a sergeant in an Indiana infantry regiment, and had won the Medal of Honor. It seems he had braved enemy fire to pull several of his comrades to safety, receiving multiple wounds in the process. He swore the marshal to secrecy, for he did not want townsfolk crowding around him asking for details—but he wanted to tell someone, and he had chosen the one person in town that would both understand the fog of combat and who could resist the urge to engage in hero-worship. After all, the marshal had to admit, everyone knows that Sam Gardner can idolize only one person at a time—either a lady he is trying to woo or, more often, himself.

Sam had initially planned to send off for a walking stick, thinking of perhaps a silver-tip or a concealed sword, but had decided to send the business to Nash. It was the least he could do; despite his self-confessed vanity, Sam Gardner believed that Joseph Nash was a greater hero than he. Besides, he liked to give his business to good Union men, wherever possible.

Sam imagined he would have to use the stick with his left hand, keeping his *main droit* free for a fast draw if necessary. The staff—that word sounded so much better than *cane*—would also give him considerably more reach than his long-barreled Colt, for subduing miscreants. He took a few practice whacks through the air to get a feel for it.

The office door opened, and his new deputy Seamus O'Connor stepped in. Sam realized, with a bit of a start, that he was going to have to stop thinking of Quint as the "new deputy" now, and advance him to the rank of "veteran" in his mind. It was a sad thought. Quint was a very capable young man, if a bit of a bore, but he was not quite the veteran that Fred Garvey had been. Sam burned with anger when he thought about the Danbys and their rampage through his town, and the loss of a man who was the closest thing he'd had in years to a friend—and the fire blazed hotter still at the knowledge that Sam had been left too wounded to ride after the bastards and bring them to justice. These thoughts inspired Sam to take one more emphatic swing at the air with his new walking stick.

"I'm sorry to be bustin' in on ye, Marshal," O'Connor said, "and you playin' with your shillelagh and all. But I found old Rupe, like you asked—he was fast asleep in Ben Tolliver's hayloft." O'Connor looked beside him, and realized he had entered alone. "Damn, he was right here."

The big deputy stepped back outside, and a moment later he re-entered holding Rupe Tingley by the scruff of the neck like a wet puppy. The two men presented a stark contrast.

Seamus O'Connor stood six feet five in his socks. His height was augmented by the battered stovepipe hat he wore; his breadth was augmented by the great red walrus mustaches that flowed from under his oft-broken nose. He had faced danger aplenty in his time, from employment as a New York City constable in Five Points to service as a first sergeant in the 63rd New York Infantry, part of the celebrated Irish Brigade, during the war. He had made his way West as a railroad worker— when he heard that a constabulary position had opened up in Wolf Creek due to the death of Fred Garvey, O'Connor had drawn his wages from the AT&SF and applied at once.

The man who dangled from O'Connor's massive paw could not have been more different. Rupe Tingley had the scrawny frame of a man who has been on a drunk for several years. There was no trace of the confidence that radiated from his Irish captor's visage; if anything, when emotion passed over Rupe's features it was most often shame. Unless thirst could be counted as an emotion, and in Rupe's case it probably could be.

Rupe's left arm was missing just below the elbow. No one knew how he had lost it, but it was a regrettably

common sight—only six years since the war had ended—
to see blind, crippled, and maimed men on the streets of
most any town. Most people didn't prod them for
particulars, and most of them didn't volunteer any. Still,
Sam couldn't help wondering if Rupe had crawled into a
bottle because of the loss of his arm—the marshal knew
many who had—or if some deeper, less visible injury had
driven him there.

"What shall I do with the darlin' man, sir?" O'Connor
asked.

"Just dump him into that chair."

The deputy did so, none too ceremoniously. Rupe still
did not wake up.

"Did you look into that incident at the Lucky Break?"
Sam asked his deputy.

O'Connor nodded. "That I did. This stranger—Hay
Bear—just took a good look at the house dealer, Jones,
and challenged him to a fancy old-fashioned duel, which
they held out by the corral. Mister Jones came out on top.
It plays that way with all the witnesses. Jones claims not
to know the fella—said he was vaguely familiar, though,
and figured he might have cleaned the man out on some
river boat somewhere."

Sam nodded. "I imagine that must happen a lot in his
business. Oh well. I suppose, busy as this town is getting,
we'll be seeing more and more daylight shootings. But
I'll let Dab know that if this gambler of his starts making
it a habit, he'll have to move on. I aim to keep a lid on
this pot and keep it from boiling over."

"All right then, Marshal," O'Connor announced. "I'll
be gettin' back to my rounds, then."

"Thanks, Seamus. I'll most likely see you around
town later this evening."

O'Connor departed, and Sam climbed to his feet and walked around his desk, to stand over Rupe. He leaned down and gave the drunk a few mild smacks on the cheek until his eyes lolled open.

"Rise and shine, Rupe."

The drunk sputtered. "Marshal—Marshal Gardner?"

"In the flesh," Sam said.

Rupe looked around. "Is there—is there a mess needs cleanin' up?" Rupe earned his drinking money by swamping the floors at various saloons, cleaning the livery stable, and sometimes sweeping up around the jail and the marshal's office—wherever someone needed a hand. But only one hand.

Sam shook his head. "Oh, there's a mess all right, and you can help me clean it up, but not like you think."

"I—I don't understand."

Sam pulled his own chair around from behind his desk, so he could sit beside Rupe.

"Let me ask you something, Rupe. I've been good to you, haven't I? Wouldn't you say I've treated you fair?"

Rupe's eyes seemed to clear after a moment, and he gained some focus. He nodded slowly.

"Oh, Lord, yes, Marshal. I reckon you've treated me better than anybody in this town. You were the first one took me in off the street, and gave me honest work—without laughing at me, or making sport. And you bein' a famous lawman, that—that kinda made it mean even more. You didn't have to be nice to me."

The marshal reflected on Rupe's words for a moment. "Well, I don't know about that last part. The higher a man goes up, the more he knows how far a man can fall. And besides that, I know people, Rupe. You have to, in this job. And I've always seen a spark in you. I'm not quite sure what it is, but it's there. There's more to you than meets the eye."

Rupe's eyes misted for a moment, then he said, "Where's that mess you wanted me to mop up, Marshal?"

Sam shook his head and smiled. "No, I need something else from you today, Rupe. I need you to tell me about last night—last night down in Cribtown. Quint found you passed out there this morning, and seems you'd been out for a good spell. What do you remember, from before you passed out? Do you know what time you got there?"

Rupe's eyes lost their focus, and he seemed dizzy. He shook his head as if he were trying to clear the cobwebs.

"Rupe? Take your time, now. Just think.

A look of horror passed over the drunk's face. He looked slowly up at Sam.

"I never—I never killed nobody, Marshal."

Sam's eyes narrowed. "I know you didn't, Rupe. I never said anything about killing anybody. Why did you say that?"

Rupe looked confused. "I don't—I ain't sure why I said that. It just, sort of, come out."

"What do you remember?"

"I don't remember anything—honest, Marshal. I'd tell you if I did. I just—there's *something*, I can't tell what it is, there's something in my mind."

Rupe squeezed his eyes tight and concentrated. His hands shook with the effort.

"I'm sorry, Marshal. I'm—I just—I *can't remember*."

Sam sighed. "It's all right, Rupe. I believe you. It'll come to you directly. But just in case you *did* see something—something you were never meant to see— well, you'd best stay here for awhile, where it's safe, while you finish sleeping it off."

Rupe looked crestfallen—quite an accomplishment, considering how low he usually was to begin with. "Are you puttin' me in jail, Sam?"

Sam stared at him for several seconds. "No, Rupe," he finally said. "You can sleep it off on my cot, in the back room. I'm going to be out, probably pretty late, it won't be an imposition to me."

To Sam's surprise, Rupe almost smiled. "Thank you, Marshal." Then a shadow passed over his face. "I hope—I hope I don't stink it up too much."

"Don't worry on that account. I'll have it cleaned—and send Dab Henry the bill." They both smiled at that.

"Get along then," Sam said. "And stay put till I send for you."

Rupe stumbled into the back room and collapsed onto the cot. In no time he was snoring deeply. He had bad dreams, dreams of terror and death, thinly disguised memories—but they had nothing to do with the previous night. They were about a previous life.

* * *

Sam decided to stop by the barber shop across the street and get a shave before he headed to the saloons. The town's only barber, John Hix, knew his business—but he had a bad habit of disappearing from town for days on end with no explanation. Sam was content to take advantage of his presence when he was around—a man could shave himself, after all, but it just didn't seem cultured.

Sam stepped inside the barber's shop and was gratified to see that no one else was waiting—the only other customer was already in the chair.

"Hello, John," Sam said. "Hello, Reverend Stone," he added, once he recognized the customer. Obadiah Stone, preacher at Wolf Creek Community Church, was a bear of a man with a thick gray-and-red beard. The thought occurred to him that the reverend and Deputy O'Connor looked like kinsmen—but even if they were, it would not deflect the Reverend Stone from loathing the abomination of O'Connor's papist beliefs.

"Howdy, Marshal," Hix said. "I'll be right with you, soon as I finish with the reverend here."

"Hello, Marshal," Stone said. "My, that is a lovely walking stick you have there!"

Sam sat down and removed his hat. "Thank you, Reverend. I know you for a man who appreciates a good walking stick."

Stone chuckled. "Mine is leaned against the corner yonder, as you can see."

Sam smiled. "Why, I did not recognize it as such; I thought it a small tree."

"I prefer to think of it as a cudgel," Stone said. "The Cudgel of the Lord, for smiting the occasional arrogant sinner."

Stone's words were not hyperbole. He was well known for rapping people lightly on the skull with his oaken cane when making a doctrinal point to them; and for rapping not-so-lightly if they got lippy. For especially extreme cases, the reverend carried a Walker Colt on his saddle and wore one of the new Smith & Wesson Model 3's on his hip.

"Lean on the Lord thy God," Reverend Stone said. "And when He needs a hand with His smiting of the wicked, why, lean into that, too, I say."

"Amen," Sam said.

"A-*men*," the barber agreed emphatically.

"Say, Reverend," Sam said, "maybe you and I can bring the quarterstaff back into style. Right out of Robin Hood. Of course, you could play Friar Tuck *or* Little John."

The preacher chuckled amiably.

"The Reverend here was just telling me about his war-time service," Hix said. "Sounds like he was a real curly wolf back then."

"Oh, you exaggerate," Stone demurred.

"You'd better get used to it, Reverend Stone," Sam said. "When it comes to the late conflict, John here has more questions than a little kid. He rummages through everybody's memories that pass by, I suspect he may be writing a military history in his spare time."

"Oh, I'm just curious, is all," Hix said. "I was out in California, around Frisco, when the war was goin' on—I feel like I missed out on somethin' important. My grandpa used to set on the front porch and talk about the War of 1812, and this was way bigger'n that'un was. So I like to hear all about it I can."

"Were you out there panning for gold?" the preacher asked.

"Oh no. I was just barberin' them that was."

Sam smiled. "I see—you were on the Barber-y Coast!"

"Huh?" Hix said, but the preacher guffawed.

"It's a joke, son," Stone explained. "A play on words. You know, the Barbary Coast—the infamous neighborhood in San Francisco?"

"Oh," Hix said, and then laughed nervously. "I'm kinda slow with them kind of jokes."

"No need to apologize, John," Sam said, "it was a silly pun."

Hix smiled. "Okay," he said. "anyway—did you know, Marshal, that the reverend was a Union cavalry officer, just like you was?"

"Why, I was unaware of this."

Stone smiled proudly. "Formerly Lieutenant-Colonel Obadiah Stone, Eighth Kentucky Cavalry, at your service, sirs."

Sam gave him a playful salute. "Former Captain Gardner, Third Illinois Cavalry, reporting. Always a pleasure to meet another Union man, especially an old horse soldier."

"I always thought it was peculiar," Hix said, "Kentucky not joining the Confederacy. Them being a slave state and all."

"I was no abolitionist, I assure you," Stone said. "I fought to preserve this grand Union of ours—my grandfather gave his life at the Battle of King's Mountain to help establish it, I did not intend to see it sundered by a motley crew of hotheaded fools."

"Here, here," Sam said in agreement.

"I hear there was a lot of guerrilla war in Kentucky, same as out here," Hix said.

The preacher harrumphed. "Irregulars. Damned useless lot, if you ask me, on either side. Skulking snakes. Nothing gave me greater pleasure, sir, than shooting down Rebel bushwhackers like the dogs they were, and the Good Lord's Arm was with me when I did it."

Hix was standing with his back to Sam, having turned the preacher's chair around to face the mirror while he finished his task. At Reverend Stone's words, the barber stiffened—almost imperceptibly—and Sam saw a shadow seem to flit across the barber's face in the mirror. In a heartbeat, though, it was gone. The marshal would have been tempted to ascribe it to squeamishness, had he not heard reports about the barber's recent bravery when the stagecoach he was on was attacked by hostile Kiowa. He decided, then, that it was lingering embarrassment that he had not had the honor to serve, and put it out of his mind.

The marshal would have been surprised indeed at the true cause of the barber's reaction. John Hix had never been to California, and had instead ridden with a band of Missouri Confederate guerrillas loosely affiliated with Quantrill—while he was absent at a prison camp, his family had paid a heavy price at the hands of Kansas Jayhawkers. He inquired about all his customers' war service, hoping to find a few former Union guerrillas and exact a bit of revenge on them. He had come across a couple in the months he had been at Wolf Creek, and after they left his barbershop he tracked them down and gave them a much closer shave than they bargained for.

John Hix smiled amiably into the mirror and spoke to the preacher. "There we are, Reverend, all done!"

Stone admired the barber's handiwork. "Very good," he said.

The preacher stood up and paid. "I hope to see both of you gentlemen at the morning services come Sunday," he said.

"I may surprise you and show up one day," Sam said, as he took the preacher's place in the barber's chair.

"I might see you," Hix said—that was always his reply, but he never meant it. On Sunday mornings, when most of his customers were in church, Hix went down to Cribtown to see a tiny but buxom whore named Haddie.

She didn't mind being slapped around a little, and after a full week of toadying to Yankee sumbitches like these he needed to blow off steam with a vengeance. *Barber-y Coast my Rebel ass,* he mused.

He draped a cloth around Sam Gardner's neck, his smile still in place.

"You ready for me to cut off them pretty curls, Marshal?"

"You know better, John. My neck would be cooler in this damn heat, but the ladies about town would no doubt lynch you for depriving them of anything worthwhile to run their fingers through. No, I only ask that you trim my goatee and give my cheeks a nice smooth shave."

"Yes, sir," Hix said, and proceeded to lather up the marshal's cheeks. Sam relaxed, closing his eyes, enjoying the sensation and the barbershop smells.

"Marshal Gardner!" a shrill voice interrupted. Sam's head jerked up—he was fortunate Hix had not yet brought out his razor.

His heart fell. It was Edith Pettigrew, the town shrew. She and her husband Seth had been among the founders of the town, almost twenty years earlier. She had always been something of a busybody, and a prude, but folks who had lived in Wolf Creek a long time told the marshal she had gotten much worse after her husband died. Sam had known for some time that her decline involved more than just an increase in self-righteousness—the rest of the town was slowly figuring that part out, as well.

She stood uncertainly in the barbershop doorway. "I apologize for intruding into this—this masculine sanctuary," she said. "But practically the only other place I can find you is in one of those foul saloons, and I refuse to even darken the doorway of one of those dens of Satan.

And it's not as though you ever actually show up at your office."

"What can I do for you, Mrs. Pettigrew?"

She looked around, conspiratorially, then spoke in a hushed tone.

"He's at it again, Marshal!"

"Who?"

"That livery man, that's who! Tolliver, or Torrance, or Tollison, or whatever he's calling himself."

"Ah," Sam said. "Yes, it is hard to follow his name changes—I've come to just think of him as 'B. T.' to simplify things in my own mind. I presume, then, that our mighty stable-master is once more baring his hirsute torso, before God and tax-paying citizens, in flagrant disregard of all civilized rules of propriety?"

"Why—why yes, that's exactly what he's doing."

"He's doing *what*?" Hix asked.

"Ben Tolliver is walking around without his shirt on again," Sam explained.

"Oh," Hix said. "Well—ain't it mighty hot in there with them horses, though, it bein' August?"

"It is mighty hot in Hell, Mister Hix," Edith Pettigrew said. "Marshal, I demand you do something. I am tired of consulting Sheriff Satterlee—he keeps telling me it is not a county problem, it is a city problem."

"Does he, now," Sam said. *Damn his eyes, I'll get him for this.*

"What are you going to do about it?"

"Madam, it is a shame you weren't here a few minutes earlier. Reverend Stone was in this very chair—I think this sort of damnable, sinful behavior is more his territory than mine."

She sniffed the air haughtily. "Sir, I am a Methodist!"

Sam leaned forward, studying the woman's face. Even from this distance he could tell that her eyes were glazed. She was chasing the dragon, all right.

"Was his shirt all the way off?" Sam asked.

"Of course!"

"The bastard!" Sam said.

"Marshal!" she gasped.

"Why, I bet he was perspiring—so heavily that his body shimmered, and his trousers dripped!"

She fanned herself. "Oh my!"

"And this took place in his stable, am I correct?"

"Of course!"

"Then, dear lady, how could you have known about it?"

"Because—because—oh!"

Sam leaned forward. "Fear not, madam," he said. "I'll take a hand in this, indeed I shall."

"What will you do?"

"I'll shoot him if I have to. But I think a stern talking to will suffice."

"I—thank you, Marshal."

"No need to thank me, it is my job. And in fact, you have stung my conscience, Mrs. Pettigrew, by pointing out as you did how prodigal I have been in my duties. As soon as I straighten this renegade wrangler out, I'll find something else productive to put my hand to—in fact, I might just get ambitious and take actions to stamp out the wicked opium trade that is going on in this city, under our very noses, and expose the criminals who are encouraging those godless Celestials by purchasing their vile wares. Thank you, madam, for inspiring me."

"I really must be going, Marshal," Edith Pettigrew said, and bustled away.

"That woman is cracked in the head," John Hix said.

"At the very least."

"Marshal—I shouldn't be spreading tales, but most ever'body knows she sends that poor afflicted boy Dickie Dildine down to the Red Chamber to buy her dope. Or, when he ain't around, that one-armed drunk."

Sam nodded. "She hasn't been pestering either of them lately, that I can tell. She must have some new way of procuring what she needs. And that's good, in my opinion. She has no business getting either of those poor souls mixed up in her antics."

"Are you really gonna close Soo Chow down, like you told her?"

"Hell, no. There's no law against opium, any more than there is against whiskey or walking around in a stable with your shirt off. Besides, I wouldn't want to cut her off. I'd be tempted to buy her supply out of my own salary, if I had to—if she's this annoying on dope, I'd hate to see what she's like without it."

Sam leaned back. "Carry on, John. The dens of Satan are calling my name."

John grinned. "Yes sir, Marshal."

* * *

Sam stepped out of the barber shop. He paused a moment, looking up and down the street. He liked to be aware of his surroundings, a habit he had picked up as a cavalry officer. He had certainly not picked it up while growing up in his hometown of Danville, Illinois—there was nothing to see there but corn, and nothing to hear but his lawyer father's boring platitudes.

He turned right and headed west down South Street. He intended to start his rounds, as he usually did, at the

Eldorado. He planned to ask around about the mysterious Laird Jenkins, the fellow who'd gotten himself shot in the back while taking a piss outside Asa's Saloon. Quint had done a thorough job earlier in the day, but there were certain townspeople who might open up more to the city marshal with the deadly reputation than to his straight-arrow deputy. And since it was now late afternoon, there might be more folks up and about who had seen Jenkins than there had been when Quint did his questioning.

The Eldorado was the most upscale drinking establishment in Wolf Creek. Its South Street location was on the border between the "respectable" part of town and the rowdy neighborhood called Dogleg City that had sprung up in the last couple of years, since the railroad arrived. It was the sort of place that local businessmen, or those passing through on the AT & SF, could feel safe frequenting, sipping a drink on cushioned barstools or doing a little gambling without the fear of being murdered if they won two hands in a row, or robbed as soon as they got out the door.

A handbill pasted on the front door advertised that the Du Pree Players would be returning next weekend. That was another marker of the sort of place Virgil Calhoun ran; Howard Du Pree and his troupe made a circuit through southern Kansas, appearing in Wolf Creek every month or so. They performed comedy skits, song and dance routines, and excerpts from Shakespeare. They didn't get booked in Dogleg City; Sam sometimes mused about how amusing it might be to see them do *Hamlet* or *Julius Caesar* at the Wolf's Den. It would be the first time they'd done the murder scenes with audience participation.

Sam opened the door and stepped inside. The house gambler—and bouncer, on the rare occasion one was required—sat at the lonely poker table, waiting for the gamblers to wake up and start stirring. The faro and monte stations—the Eldorado only ran three tables—sat empty. The dealer, Tom Scroggins, was a rough-looking character with long black hair and a grizzled goatee—one could argue he was an unkempt version of the marshal, at least in appearance.

"Looks like the place is getting a slow start today, eh, Tom?" Sam said as he walked past.

Scroggins shrugged. "It's okay, Marshal. I'm a bit of a slow starter myself, anyhow."

Sam chuckled. "Things'll pick up when the dance hall girls get started. A little flash of female leg gets folks' blood flowing."

The piano player had arrived, and was limbering his fingers up at the keyboard. Sven Larson was the best piano man in town; Sam didn't bother asking him any questions, the Minnesotan got completely lost in his music once he got started, and would not likely have noticed if the whole place collapsed around his ears.

Instead, he bellied up to the bar and ordered a beer. Head bartender Robert Sutton set a foamy mug before him. The marshal and Sutton got along quite well, being fellow Illinois escapees. The bartender—a thin man around sixty with a snow white beard and a toothy grin—hailed from Urbana, and had spent the war years as a guard at the Rock Island prison camp. Affable as he was, he had no compunction about using the shotgun hidden behind the bar if it were necessary. Gardner joked that having a bartender named Robert at the Eldorado, when there was a bartender named Rob at the Lucky Break, was far too confusing for the simple folk of Wolf Creek, so the marshal sometimes referred to them as Smilin' Bob and Burly Rob.

"How's that leg doing, Sam?" Smilin' Bob Sutton asked.

The marshal set his mug down. "The doc says it's coming along well. I shouldn't need this walking stick for long, now that I'm finally on my feet—but it's so dandy and handy, I may just make it a permanent part of my arsenal. Joseph Nash does good work."

"Hey, that's a beaut," Sutton said. "Can I see it?"

Sam handed it over and the bartender appraised it with an approving smile.

"Say, Bob," the marshal said. "I guess you heard about the fellow who got shot down in Cribtown last night."

Sutton nodded. "Quint was asking about him this morning. I really can't tell you much—he just came in here a few times in the early evening, had a couple of drinks and moved on."

"I hear he was a bit of a talker."

Sutton shook his head. "Not so's I'd notice, not in here. I'd say this was where he started his evening's festivities, and he hadn't drunk enough yet to loosen his tongue till somewhere farther down the line."

Sam nodded. "If you don't mind, I'm going to pester your customers about him just the same."

Sutton handed the cane back. "Sure thing, Sam."

There weren't that many customers to pester, not at this hour. Sam knew most of them—and they proved as unhelpful as Sutton—but then a man entered who was a stranger to him. He was in his forties, wearing a cheap, rumpled suit and a dusty bowler. He carried a leather case. The man headed straight to the bar, and Sam excused himself from the conversation he was having with a local cattleman to go join him.

"Robert," the man said to the bartender, "has Mister Calhoun come in yet?"

Sutton shook his head. "Afraid not. He should be along soon, though."

The man seemed disappointed. "Do you know if he's given any thought to my offer?"

Sutton smiled. "I'm just the hired help, you'll have to ask him about that."

Sam approached the man. "Virgil keeps the hours of a raccoon," he said, "much like the rest of us. My name is Sam Gardner, I'm the marshal around here."

"Have I done something, Marshal?"

Sam smiled. "Not that I'm aware of. I just like to make new acquaintances."

"Oh," the man said, but he did not seem relieved. "My name is Malchius Offerman." He offered his hand, and the marshal shook it.

"Mister Offerman is a whiskey drummer," Sutton offered. "He's trying to convince Virgil to change suppliers."

"I thought I knew all the whiskey drummers who come through," Sam said, and then added, "I like whiskey, you see."

Offerman nodded. "I'm new," he said. "Well, not new to the trade, just new to this territory. I replaced Lester Weatherby."

"Weatherby," Sam said, and thought a moment. "Oh, yes. He was on that stagecoach that the Kiowas hit a few weeks back."

The drummer nodded again. "I hear he quit and moved back East."

"A good place for him, from what I saw," Sam said. "Well, I wish you luck with Virgil."

"Thank you, Marshal."

"Long as I have you here, I wonder if I could ask you a question."

"Why, certainly. I always like to be helpful to the law."

"There's a fellow that has been making the rounds of the saloons the last few nights—Laird Jenkins. Dressed like a cattle drover, had a pock-marked face."

Offerman nodded. "Why, yes," he said. "I remember the man. We spoke last night, very briefly, at the Lucky Break. Is he in some sort of trouble?"

"His troubles are pretty much over. Somebody shot him in the back down in Cribtown last night."

"Oh, my," Offerman said. "That's terrible. I have been warned not to go down there too late at night, I hear it is crawling with cutthroats and robbers. No offense, Marshal, you can't be everywhere at once, I suppose."

"He wasn't robbed," Sam said, "that's the peculiar part. He had a pocket full of cash when we found him."

"Perhaps he offended someone?"

"Perhaps," Sam said. "May I ask what you talked about with him?"

"Nothing, really," Offerman said, "we barely spoke. He was rather far along in his cups, I'm afraid, and was soliciting my opinion about keno. I told him I was unfamiliar with the game. That was about the extent of it, apart from some drunken mumbling I couldn't decipher."

Sam nodded. "Thanks for your time, Mister Offerman. Bob, I believe I'll amble over to the Wolf's

Den and see how they've been getting along today without my presence—I expect I'll be back after supper. Good day, gentlemen."

Sam headed south on Third Street, tapping the boardwalk jauntily with his walking stick as he went. He walked past Li Wong's laundry shop, and caught a glimpse of Li's beautiful daughter Jing Jing through the window. The marshal generally ignored the Chinese unless they were causing trouble—they were sort of in the background, from his perspective, rather like squirrels—but he could definitely see why so many of the men in town were panting after her. If Soo Chow ever did manage to recruit her for his stable, the marshal would make a point of giving her a try.

He turned left onto Grant Street, which the mostly-Texan cowboys preferred to call "Useless S. Grant." Let them have their sour grapes, Sam figured, everyone knows who won the war and was sitting in the White House. He passed the artist, Reginald de Courcey, headed back to his studio—brushes and canvas under his arm—no doubt from one of his frequent sketching and painting expeditions in the countryside.

"Hello, Marshal," the artist said amiably in his proper English accent. "Warm enough for you?"

"I suppose it'll do," Sam said. "How's business?"

"A little slow right now—but I'm using the downtime to paint some landscapes that I suspect I can get a pretty penny for the next time I get to Wichita. Have a good evening!"

"Same to you."

The Wolf's Den was geographically not that far from the Eldorado, but it was worlds away. Everything about it felt different, even in the late afternoon. Where Tom

Scroggins was friendly, and pleasant company on a slow evening, Breedlove's house gambler Preston Vance radiated a taciturn, antisocial aura. Three or four toughs lounged around the bar at night, ready at a moment's notice to subdue any serious troublemakers—one of them, a drifter named Wesley Quaid, was already present. Instead of Sven Larson's jaunty piano, the young Texan Roscoe Parsons played Mexican tunes on a guitar.

And Ira Breedlove watched over it all from the end of the bar. Ira lived in an upstairs room, and almost never left the property—but his web extended all over town.

He stood there now, and Sam joined him.

"Ira," the marshal said in greeting.

"Sam. I see you're getting around well." Ira did not look at the marshal directly—it was more a dismissive than an anxious gesture.

"Well enough. Better than Laird Jenkins."

Sam watched Breedlove carefully, hoping for a reaction, but received none.

"Mister Jenkins got himself backshot last night," Sam added.

"So I heard."

"No one seems to know much about him," Sam said. "Except Asa Pepper seems to think he was working for you."

"Really."

"Oh yes, really. Normally I wouldn't trust Asa as far as I could throw his black ass—but he's not stupid. He certainly wouldn't kill somebody right outside his place and just leave him there. Though he may have had reason to—he thinks Jenkins was there to pressure him about paying back a loan you apparently floated him."

Ira turned his head to stare at the marshal. "And what do *you* think, Sam?"

Sam shrugged. "I don't have enough facts to think anything. Dab seems to believe I'm wasting time and stirring up trouble even investigating this murder. Do you feel that way?"

Ira let out a small sigh. "Laird was an old friend of mine," he said. "From my St. Louis days. He was a confidence man, for the most part—he didn't pressure people, he didn't need to. He *convinced* them, usually over a little time."

Breedlove took a pre-rolled cigarette out of a silver case he kept in his vest pocket, and lit it. Sam remained silent, letting the saloon owner go through his ritual. After a few puffs of smoke, Ira continued.

"Laird came in here a few days ago, asking for work for old time's sake. He wanted to get out to Santa Fe, and needed a stake—despite his avocation, he was not the sort of man who'd accept a loan as a favor, he'd want to earn it somehow."

"So you sent him around Asa's?"

Ira nodded. "It wasn't to get the loan paid off, though. I had an offer for Asa—but I didn't want to make it straight off, I wanted to soften him up a little first. Let him know I was watching him, give him something to think about."

"But you didn't want anyone else to know," Sam said. "So your man Laird didn't go straight to Asa. He spent a few days making the rounds of saloons, spending a little time in each, to throw your competitors off the trail. And he was perfect, because if you sent one of your regular cronies it would attract too much attention."

"Something like that."

Sam chuckled. "Must've been a hell of a plan you were cooking up, to take that much trouble in how you went about it."

Ira half-smiled. "Laird was going to make the real offer to Asa tonight. In return for a cut of the profits, I was going to start directing our girls' overflow customers to Asa. I wasn't calling in the loan, I was going to offer him another one, to hire more whores. After awhile I would be willing to accept a half-interest in the place as repayment of the loans."

"Why are you telling me all this?"

"Because I'm still going to do it. And you have a stake in that sort of business, so it'll affect you."

Sam shook his head appreciatively. "Damn, Ira," he said. "There's only so many horny men in this town."

Ira smiled. "The town is growing. There'll be more."

"And if you expand, and bring Asa's operation into your own—that'll give you the leverage to cut the others out. Abby Potter, Dab Henry, Soo Chow, even Virgil Calhoun, though he's discreet about it. There's a lot of people selling ass in this town."

"Wouldn't it be simpler if there were fewer?" Ira said. "Abby would do fine, she caters to the more established business folk, not the drovers. And Soo Chow doesn't have that many whores—it just makes sense to have a few Oriental girls around when you're selling dope."

"So it's mostly Dab Henry and Virgil Calhoun you'd be trying to drive out of business."

Ira shrugged. "You'd get the same cut, no matter who gave it to you."

"It's not the money, Ira. The way I figure it, I'm entitled to a little bonus for keeping everything running smooth around here. But my real job is keeping the peace, and you and the others are edging closer and closer to a war. It's already starting—this is just the kind of shit I don't like. Somebody figured out what your amigo Laird was up to. Hell, I've had two shootings in one day. If that keeps up it hurts everybody."

Ira nodded, and smiled. "I heard about that little duel at Dab's place."

Realization dawned on Sam's face. "I'll be damned," he said. "You had something to do with that."

"I have no idea what you're talking about."

"It doesn't matter."

Ira's brow furrowed. "Sam, do you know the real reason I'm telling you all this?"

"I'm sure you're about to inform me."

"Laird was my friend. And he died working for me. I do want you to get to the bottom of it."

"So I can maybe put the heat on one of your rivals."

"So you can do what's right," Ira said.

Sam sighed. "I probably *should* just drop the whole thing. It's going to be nothing but trouble."

"But you won't," Ira said. "Because you're not that sort of man. Your young deputy wanders around Dogleg City, acting like Sir Lancelot, well meaning but naïve as a church mouse. You're more worldly, but you have a streak of the same thing in you."

Ira smiled at him, but not with his eyes.

Sam stared back. "You may be right," he said. "But that streak, as you call it, applies to how I treat everybody. You'd best not forget it."

"Oh, I won't. I never forget anything, Sam, you know that."

"It's time for me to go procure my supper," Sam said, after a few uncomfortable moments. "I'll be back tonight."

"I'll be here."

Sam left the saloon, headed for Isabella's restaurant. Ira Breedlove turned to face the bar, cupped his chin in his right hand, and was soon lost in thought.

CHAPTER FOUR

Some men were born to step in shit as they went about the business of earning their daily bread.

Ira Breedlove was not one of them.

Ira had come to that realization at an early age. He had been so young when his father Tobias came west from Missouri to establish a cattle spread that Ira didn't remember any childhood home other than the T Bar B. He didn't remember his mother at all, since she had died giving birth to him.

Because of that loss, Ira had been raised by a crusty old cattleman and a crew of wild young cowhands, and he had seen with his own eyes how hard they worked— from dawn to dusk, from can to can't, most days—and how dirty and smelly they always were. He hadn't been very old when he realized that such a life was not for him. When his father suggested sending him to St. Louis to complete his education, Ira had agreed to the idea without hesitation. He knew what Tobias had in mind. The old man figured Ira would come back to the ranch when his schooling was done and take over running the T Bar B, and he would be able to do a better job of that if he knew more things.

Ira had learned plenty of things in St. Louis, but how to run a ranch successfully hadn't been included in his chosen curriculum.

"You want a drink, boss?"

The question broke into Ira's musings. It came from Mack, the bartender on duty at the moment, who had seen the owner of the Wolf's Den leaning on the bar and figured maybe he was thirsty. It was a reasonable assumption.

Ira straightened from his casual pose and shook his head. "Not right now."

"Couple of the girls ain't busy. You could take one of 'em up to your room if you was of a mind to."

Anger surged through Ira. He put both hands on the bar, glared at the bartender, and said, "Of course I can take one of those whores upstairs if I want to. They work for me, after all."

"Sure, boss, sure," Mack said, quick to try to soothe Ira's ruffled feelings. Everybody who worked at the Wolf's Den knew it was a good idea not to get Ira Breedlove mad. "I just thought you looked a mite . . . pensive, is all."

"Pensive?" Ira's anger evaporated, at least the momentary annoyance he had felt at the bartender, and was replaced by curiosity. "Where did you learn a word like that?"

"Read it in a book, boss. Fella went off and left it in here one day, and I started to throw it away but then I thought, hell, I might as well read it. I had a little schoolin' when I was a kid, but I don't get to put it to much use workin' here, you know."

"No, the Wolf's Den isn't exactly what you'd call a bastion of culture, is it?"

"I wouldn't call it any sort of a name like that, boss. I like workin' here."

"Good, good." Ira lightly slapped a palm on the hardwood. "If anybody's looking for me, I'll be in the office."

"Sure thing, boss."

Ira went through a door at the end of the bar. Behind it was a short passage with another door on each side. The one on the right led into a storage room where crates of liquor and other supplies were stacked. The left-hand door opened into the small office where Ira kept a desk. He had another desk upstairs in his living quarters and did most of his accounting up there, but he liked having a place down here where he could get away from the barroom for a few minutes without having to climb all the way to the second floor.

The room had a single window covered by a yellow curtain. The pane was open a few inches at the moment, but there wasn't much breeze. The curtain stirred every now and then, but only a little.

Ira sat down at the desk and unlocked one of the drawers. He made sure there was always a bottle of decent whiskey behind the bar for his personal use, but when he really wanted something better to drink he came here. He was the only one who knew about the bottle of cognac in the drawer. He took out a glass along with it and poured a couple of fingers of the smooth, fiery liquor. After replacing the cork in the bottle, he lifted the glass, and even though he was alone in the office, he spoke aloud as he said, "Here's to you, Laird . . . and to St. Louis."

* * *

—Twelve years earlier—

The Birdcage was the fanciest whorehouse in town, catering to men who had plenty of money to spend. That suited Ira, because his father provided him with a generous allowance, and it suited his friend Laird Jenkins because men with money were Laird's favorite targets for his schemes.

Some confidence men liked to prey on lonely women, but as Laird had explained to Ira, that didn't hardly seem fair to him. A woman aching for the touch of a man just couldn't think straight enough to watch out for her own best interests.

Ira suspected that such women didn't provide enough of a challenge for his friend. To Laird Jenkins, bilking folks out of their hard-earned cash wasn't just a way of earning a living. It was also a game.

At the moment, Laird had a carpetbag full of phony stock certificates he was selling, but his actual stock in trade was his ability to convince people to believe whatever he told them about how rich he was going to make them. Eventually his marks would catch on and realize he was selling a lot more certificates than there was stock to go around, but by the time that happened he would be long gone from St. Louis.

"Knowing when the hand is played out," Laird had said to Ira more than once. "Developing an instinct for that awareness is the most important skill a man can learn. Whether it's romancing a woman or skinning a mark, know when it's time to take your leave."

Of course, they didn't have to worry about that here at the Birdcage, Ira thought. Laird wasn't working tonight, and romance didn't apply in a whorehouse. The two young men were out for an evening's entertainment, that's all.

A stocky, gray-haired Negro in servant's livery met them just inside the door and took their hats. "Good evening, Mister Breedlove, Mister Jenkins," he said in a deep, cultured voice. "I trust you young gentlemen are doing well."

"We're doing splendidly, Thaddeus," Laird said, grinning. "But I expect to be doing even better soon if Mademoiselle Jessica is available."

"She is unaccompanied at the moment, I believe," the butler replied.

"How about Marcelline?" Ira asked. She was a particular favorite of his, a lithe, blond-haired beauty who was blessed with the ability to bend and twist her body in all sorts of intriguing ways.

Thaddeus winced slightly at Ira's question. "Sad to say, Mister Ira, Marcelline is with a guest at the moment. If you'd care to wait—"

A man who bedded down with whores, even the most high-class ones, didn't have any business getting upset with the idea of them being with other men. Ira knew that, but he felt a flash of annoyance, anyway. It was more a matter of impatience than fastidiousness. When he wanted something, he didn't like to wait for it, and it had been a while since he'd visited Marcelline.

"Or perhaps if you'd prefer the company of one of the other young ladies—" Thaddeus continued.

Ira shook his head. "I'll wait," he said. "Bring me something to drink in the parlor. Cognac."

"Of course, sir," Thaddeus murmured.

The two young men went into the elegantly furnished parlor, which was lit by two crystal chandeliers that cast their warm glow over plush red curtains, walls covered with brocaded paper, several spindly-legged tables, and a number of heavy, comfortable divans and armchairs. A massive stone fireplace with a gleaming mahogany mantle took up almost one entire wall of the room, and a pianoforte sat against the other wall. No one had ever played the musical instrument while Ira was here, but he presumed it was for more than just show.

Several attractive young women in various forms of skimpy attire that left little of their beauty to the imagination lounged around the parlor. One of them, a tall, slender, but well-endowed redhead stood up when Ira and Laird entered the room and came over to them. "Laird," she said as she held out both hands, "it's so good to see you again."

Laird took her hands, then pulled her into his arms and kissed her. He smacked her bottom through the thin, translucent shift she wore, and that prompted a laugh from her as they broke the kiss.

"I think you're glad to see me, too," she said.

"More than you know."

"Oh—" Jessica giggled. "I doubt that."

Laird put an arm around her shoulders and turned her toward the foyer and the winding staircase that led up to the second floor where the girls' rooms were located. He looked back at his companion and said, "I'll see you later, Ira."

Ira nodded somewhat gloomily and said, "I'll be here." Laird was going off to have his fun, and he was stuck waiting for Marcelline. The wait might well be worth it, but it still bothered him.

One of the other girls approached him when Laird and Jessica were gone. She was a brunette, pretty enough but already developing the hardness around her eyes and mouth that all whores got if they stayed in the business long enough. With some it didn't really take very long.

"I'd be glad to go upstairs with you, Mister Breedlove," she offered.

Ira shook his head. "No, that's all right . . ." His voice trailed off as he couldn't recall her name.

"Susan."

"That's right. Susan. I'll wait for Marcelline."

"She don't have . . . I mean, she doesn't have anything I don't have, Mister Breedlove."

Other than breeding and class, or at least what passed for same in such an environment, thought Ira. Still, he put a polite smile on his face as he shook his head and said, "I don't think so, but thank you anyway."

Susan was about to say something else, opening her mouth and revealing teeth that were starting to go bad, when Thaddeus bustled into the parlor carrying a silver tray with a snifter of cognac on it.

"You run along and leave Mister Ira alone," he told the brown-haired whore sharply. Susan glared daggers at him but turned and sashayed back to the divan where she joined two other girls in waiting for the next customer.

Thaddeus handed the snifter to Ira.

"There you go, sir," he said.

"Thanks." Ira took a coin from his coat pocket and tossed it to the servant, who plucked it deftly from the air. Thaddeus, Marcelline had told Ira once, was a runaway slave from Louisiana who had made his way upriver to St. Louis and pretended to be a freedman. He had phony manumission papers he had gotten hold of somehow, and since he was able to read, a skill not many blacks had, he had taught himself how to speak like an educated man, too. Ira wasn't sure how Thaddeus had wound up working for Rose Delacroix, the woman who owned the Birdcage, nor did he care.

The butler tucked the coin away, held the silver tray at his side, and nodded. "I shall inform you as soon as Miss Marcelline is available, sir," he said.

Ira nodded, and Thaddeus turned and left the parlor. Ira took a sip of the cognac and appreciated the liquor's fine, smooth bite. Marcelline had introduced him to cognac, and there was nothing to compare with it in the saloons of Wolf Creek.

The whores out there in the settlement on the Kansas plains didn't compare, either. Out there a man had to settle for rotgut whiskey that might well have been brewed with rattlesnake heads and black powder in it, along with plain-faced or even downright ugly soiled doves who pulled up their skirts and lay there as unresponsive as a sack of flour while a man took care of his business. That was fine for a young cowboy who only cared about losing his innocence, but Ira preferred a woman who was more skilled in the amatory arts.

From time to time, Ira thought that a man who opened a saloon providing good liquor and a better class of prostitute would make a lot of money in a place like Wolf Creek. He had toyed with the idea of doing just that when his father finally made him come home.

But the reality of the situation was that cognac and women like Marcelline would be wasted on the denizens of Wolf Creek. They were too crude to fully appreciate either one. If he ever opened a saloon, he would give those frontiersmen exactly what they deserved, no more, no less.

The best things in life, he would save for himself.

Susan was at his elbow again, he realized as he sipped the liquor. "Marcelline's gonna—going to be upstairs for quite a while, I'll bet," the brunette said. "That fella who went with her was bellowing about how he'd been saving up his lovin' for a long, long time."

Ira was irritated because he knew Susan was just trying to cajole him into giving her his business, instead of Marcelline. "I don't mind waiting," he snapped, even though he did mind. He minded a lot.

"She might even need to take a bath when she's done with him," Susan went on. "He stunk to high heaven. Of course, you might not care about that."

Ira knew he shouldn't give in to his curiosity, but he asked, "What sort of man was he?" Gentlemen patronized the Birdcage, for the most part, but the brothel wouldn't turn away any man who had the money to afford the price.

"He was a big man, with a beard and long, tangled hair," Susan said. "He wore buckskins and a hat with a brim out to here." She indicated the dimensions of the wide brim with her hands. "He had a pair of revolvers stuck behind his belt, and the biggest knife I've ever seen in a sheath with fringe on it."

"Sounds like a fur trapper," Ira commented. That was a dying business, but he had seen some of the old mountain men from time to time, both back in Wolf Creek and here in St. Louis. Actually, they were more common here in St. Louis because the fur companies had their headquarters here and the trappers would bring in loads of pelts to sell.

Susan said, "I think he must have been. He stank of death, I know that."

95

That was a dramatic thing to say, thought Ira. He didn't know whether to believe Susan or not. She was capable of making up this yarn on the spot, just to try to steal a customer from Marcelline. More than likely, the gent who'd taken Marcelline upstairs was some mild-mannered businessman.

That thought had just crossed Ira's mind when a gravelly voice roared like a wounded grizzly bear, "Come back here, you damned whore!"

All eyes in the parlor turned toward the foyer as a frightened scream followed hard on the heels of the angry bellow. A young woman with long blond hair streaming down her back fled down the staircase, as naked as the day she was born. Close behind her loomed a massive figure, giving chase.

The man towered several inches over six feet and had shoulders seemingly as broad as an ax handle. He was bare from the waist up, revealing a thickly muscled chest covered with a rusty red pelt. His beard and the tangled thatch of hair on his head were the same rusty shade. He wore only a pair of buckskin trousers and had a piece of rope tied around his waist as a belt. A fringed sheath hung from that rope, and the bone handle of a knife jutted up from it.

Ira started toward the foyer. He knew the blonde; in fact, she was the one he was waiting for. His lips formed the name *Marcelline*.

She was almost at the bottom of the stairs when her pursuer caught her. His ham-like hand reached out and grabbed Marcelline's long hair. She cried out again as he jerked back. Her feet went out from under her and she fell on the stairs, landing heavily.

"Marcelline!" Ira shouted as he reached the arched door between the parlor and the foyer.

The big man's head turned toward him. The lips under that forest of red hair curved in a cruel smile. "Stay back, you damned dandy," the man said, "or I'll twist your head right off your shoulders. They call me Cougar, and it's my night to howl!"

Marcelline's tumble had stunned her. She moaned weakly as the giant trapper wrapped his fingers around her arm and hauled her to her feet as if she were weightless. She muttered, "No—no—"

"I done bought and paid for your time, gal," Cougar said. "You'll do whatever I want with no complaints. A whore ain't got no business bein' so dadblasted persnickety!"

Ira's pulse hammered inside his skull. He wanted to help Marcelline, but the brute that had hold of her was huge and clearly vicious. Didn't Rose Delacroix employ men to deal with situations like this?

Thaddeus appeared through a door on the other side of the foyer and pointed a sawed-off shotgun at Cougar. "Release the young woman!" he ordered. "If you don't, I'll have no choice but to fire."

Cougar's eyes, set deep in pits of leathery gristle, opened wider for a second. No man could stare down the twin barrels of a shotgun without feeling some fear. But then it went away and he laughed.

"Go ahead and shoot," he taunted Thaddeus. "But if you pull them triggers, you'll splatter the whore all over these stairs, too."

Ira's hope for Marcelline's rescue fell as he realized the trapper was right. The buckshot would be equally deadly to her.

As it turned out, though, Thaddeus was just trying to delay Cougar until help arrived. A big man in wool trousers and a homespun shirt came running up behind him, and another man about the same size appeared at the top of the stairs. They were the Birdcage's real bodyguards and bouncers.

The man at the top of the stairs carried a leather, shot-filled sap. The other clutched a short, stout club. They charged at Cougar from both directions at the same time.

Cougar dealt with the closer threat by shoving Marcelline bodily into the man below him on the stairs. They collided, their feet tangled, and they went down in a welter of flailing limbs. Cougar turned to meet the charge of the man coming from above. Moving with surprising speed for a man of his bulk, the trapper bent at the waist as the bouncer swung the sap at his head. The blow missed him, and he drove himself up a step, lowering a shoulder and ramming it into the mid-section of the off-balance bouncer.

With a roar of effort, Cougar straightened and lifted the man off his feet. Twisting, the trapper levered the bouncer up and over the banister that ran along the edge of the curving staircase. The man let out a yell of alarm that was cut off sharply as he crashed down on his back, landing on the foyer's hardwood floor.

The first bouncer thrust Marcelline's nude, limp form off of him and struggled to get his feet under him again. Just as he came upright, Cougar pivoted toward him and kicked him in the face. The trapper's feet were bare, but that didn't make much difference. Ira thought the sole of Cougar's foot looked to be as thick as if it were made of boot leather.

The kick sent the bouncer flying backward. Thaddeus scrambled to get out of the way, but he was too late. The bouncer rammed into him and knocked him off his feet. As Thaddeus sat down hard, the shotgun in his hands went off with a deafening boom. The double load of buckshot chewed a gaping hole in the fancy, flowery wallpaper and the wall boards underneath. If anybody had been on the other side of that wall, they had probably caught some of the buckshot, too, Ira thought.

Susan and the other whores in the parlor had scattered, not wanting to be anywhere near this trouble. Nor was there any sign of the whores who were upstairs when the ruckus broke out, or of their customers. They didn't want any part of what was going on. The two bouncers appeared to be either unconscious or dead, and Thaddeus couldn't be expected to stop a monster like Cougar.

That left Ira.

He was no brawler, and Cougar had several inches and fifty or sixty pounds on him. He wouldn't stand a chance and he knew it.

He took a step forward, anyway, as Cougar grabbed one of Marcelline's bare ankles and started dragging her up the stairs.

Ira's foot bumped against something that rolled on the floor. He glanced down and saw the bludgeon that the second bouncer had carried. The man had dropped it when Cougar kicked him in the face and knocked him out.

Ira didn't think about what he was doing. He stooped, snatched up the club, and charged across the foyer. He yelled incoherently as he started up the stairs.

Cougar dropped Marcelline's leg, said, "All right, you damned fool," and leaped over her to tackle Ira, who held the club in both hands and brought it down on Cougar's back as hard as he could. The trapper didn't even seem to feel the blow. He slammed Ira against the wall along the staircase with bone-jarring force. Ira's vision spun crazily. He smashed the club against Cougar's head.

As they both rebounded from the wall, Cougar tripped over Marcelline's sprawled form. Since both of his long, brawny arms were wrapped around Ira's torso, when Cougar fell, Ira went with him. They toppled down the stairs.

Thankfully, the fall was a relatively short one. When they hit the floor at the base of the stairs, the impact jolted them apart. Ira already felt like Cougar had almost squeezed him in two. His ribs ached, and his lungs cried out for air. He rolled onto his side and gasped a couple of breaths before he started trying to fight his way back to his feet.

He never had a chance to get up. Cougar's thick-fingered hands grabbed the back of his coat and lifted him into the air like a doll. Ira yelled as Cougar carried him into the parlor, raised him even higher, and flung him onto one of the tables. The spindly legs snapped under his weight and collapsed, dumping him on the rug among the debris of the broken table.

"I'm gonna stomp you until your guts come out your ears," Cougar said in his gravelly voice. To Ira's stunned brain, the words sounded like they were coming from far, far away, but he heard them clearly enough to understand them. And judging from everything he had seen so far, Cougar was more than capable of making good on that threat.

100

Knowing that his life was in danger, Ira forced his muscles to work. He grabbed one of the broken table legs, rolled over, and thrust up with it. The jagged end went into Cougar's groin. The trapper howled in pain.

Ira didn't have enough strength behind the thrust to make it penetrate very far, though. It hurt Cougar and enraged him even more, but it didn't come anywhere close to incapacitating him. Cougar swatted the table leg aside.

"Just for that, I'm gonna make you pay, boy," he said as he reached for the bone handle of his knife and dragged the weapon out of its sheath. Ira had never seen a bigger, more sinister blade in his life. Cougar continued, "This here is a Arkansas Toothpick, and I'm gonna use it to peel ever' bit of skin off you. You'll be screamin' and beggin' for me to kill you afore I'm done with you."

Frozen with horror, Ira didn't doubt that one bit.

But as Cougar held the knife in his right hand and reached for Ira with his left, something loomed up behind the trapper, rising into the air and then coming down with shattering force on Cougar's head. At the last second, Ira recognized the object as the top of the broken table. It cracked into two pieces as the blow landed with enough impact to drive Cougar to his knees.

Ira caught a glimpse of Laird Jenkins standing there and knew that his friend had struck the blow with the table, saving him—at least for the moment. But Cougar was still conscious and still a deadly threat, even on his knees. Ira drew his legs up and kicked, driving both heels into Cougar's fur-matted chest. The trapper went over backward. The Arkansas Toothpick slipped from his hand.

Ira lunged, got his fingers around the knife's handle, and lifted it. He had used knives before, but never one this heavy. The weapon had superb balance, though, which helped Ira lift it. He planted a knee in Cougar's stomach and brought the tip of the blade to rest on the big man's throat under the jutting beard.

"Don't!" Cougar croaked. "I give—"

Ira rammed down with the knife. It was razor-sharp and glided into Cougar's neck. Ira felt a second of resistance as the blade struck Cougar's spine, but it sliced on through and didn't stop until the point embedded itself in the hardwood floor. With a grotesque, gurgling sigh, Cougar's arms and legs splayed out and he went limp.

In the silence that followed, Laird said, "You killed him. He was trying to surrender."

Ira didn't look up. He kept on staring into Cougar's dead eyes. Sweat dripped from Ira's face. One of the drops fell into Cougar's left eye. He didn't blink.

"Of course I killed him," Ira said. "You think I wanted a crazy animal like that walking around holding a grudge against me?"

For a second, Laird didn't say anything. Then he chuckled and said, "You've been listening when I talk, haven't you? You recognized that the moment had come to end it."

Ira didn't respond to that. He wrenched the knife free from the floor and pulled it out of the dead man's neck. He stood up, a little shaky on his feet but growing stronger, and bent down to wipe the bloody blade on one leg of Cougar's buckskin trousers. Ira hesitated, then cut the rope belt around the trapper's waist and pulled the fringed sheath from it.

"Souvenir?" Laird asked dryly.

"I figure I earned it." Ira looked at his friend. "Thanks for saving my life, by the way."

Laird shrugged. "It goes against the grain to risk my own life to help someone else, but hell—it seemed like the thing to do at the time."

"I won't forget it," Ira promised. He looked over at Thaddeus, who was still sitting down but had scooted back against the foyer wall. "Am I going to have trouble with the law over this?"

Thaddeus swallowed and shook his head. "No, sir. We'll clean everything up, and once those two worthless cretins come to, they'll dispose of the body. I don't think anyone is likely to miss the late—gentleman."

"And you'll look after Marcelline?"

Thaddeus looked over at the blonde, who was curled up on the stairs, moaning. "We'll attend to any injuries she has, Mister Breedlove," the butler promised. "You can be assured of that."

Ira nodded and said, "Thanks." He tucked the Arkansas Toothpick under his coat. "Let's get out of here."

Laird said, "You don't want to—"

"Not in the mood anymore."

"I can't say as I blame you." As they started for the door, Laird took a cheroot from his vest pocket and put it in his mouth at a jaunty angle. "I finished with Jessica, you know. Before I came downstairs to see what all the commotion was about, I mean."

"I guess it's a good thing for me you don't give a damn about satisfying a woman, only yourself," Ira said as they went out into the night.

Laird laughed as they walked back to the carriage that had brought them to the Birdcage.

* * *

Ira could still hear that laughter in his head as he sat in the little office off the main room of the Wolf's Den, sipping cognac. He reached down to his left hip and let his fingers brush over the bone handle of the Arkansas Toothpick he had used to kill Cougar that night. He had killed other men with that blade since then, when he had to, but that one had been special.

Cougar was the first man whose life Ira Breedlove had taken.

Cougar's death had taught Ira that he could kill when it was necessary, without hesitation, without remorse, without losing a damned second of sleep over what he had done. It was a valuable lesson, quite probably the most valuable one he had learned during his "education" in St. Louis.

Ira came to a decision and tossed back the rest of the cognac that was in the glass. He stood up and went to the door, opening it to call to the bartender, "Send somebody to find Rattlesnake Jake and tell him to come see me."

"Right now, boss?"

"No, I want you to wait until the grass grows under your feet," Ira said. "Yes, right now, damn it!"

He retreated into the office as the bartender gulped and hurried to carry out his orders. Ira settled down behind the desk again and reached for the bottle. There was no doubt in his mind that Dab Henry had had something to do with Laird's death. It was unlikely that the mayor had pulled the trigger himself—Dab wouldn't want to get that much blood on his hands – but he knew how and why Laird had died. Ira intended to see to it that Dab paid for that. It might be a long campaign, but Ira had a good idea for the opening salvo.

Of course, there was usually no profit in revenge, he reminded himself as he poured another drink. He was sorry that Laird was dead, and it would be fine with him if the local law got the bottom of it, as he had told Sam Gardner.

But Ira didn't have much faith in the law. He had circumvented it himself often enough to know just how inefficient those star packers could be. If Gardner and his deputies traced Laird's murder back to Dab Henry, all well and good.

One way or another, though, Ira meant to see to it that Henry paid the price. Whether there was profit involved or not, some debts just couldn't be put aside.

* * *

Rattlesnake Jake didn't knock on the door. He opened it and came into the office. If anyone else had done that, Ira would have been angered enough to throw the intruder right back out. He was willing to give Jake some latitude, though, because the bounty hunter was probably the only person Ira knew who was as dangerous as he was.

Rattlesnake Jake had been coming and going through Wolf Creek since the war ended. He had made the Wolf's Den his unofficial headquarters when he was in town. Ira knew absolutely nothing about the man's background, not even his last name—it seemed that no one else in town did, either. Jake wore a flat-crowned black hat and a black duster over nondescript range clothes. He carried a Colt Navy on his hip. The one oddity about his garb was that he preferred shoes, heavy brogans in his case, to the boots most men wore.

"You wanted to see me, Mister Breedlove?" Jake asked. As usual, his face and voice gave away nothing.

Ira waved toward the room's other chair, but Jake gave a curt shake of the head, indicating that he wasn't interested in sitting down.

"In the past I've given you a few tips on men you might be interested in looking into," Ira began.

"And you never even asked for a cut of the price on their heads," Jake said. "That's sporting of you."

Ira smiled, but the expression was a cold one. "Why, Jake, if I didn't know any better, I might suspect that you just made a joke." He leaned forward. "But that's neither here nor there. I'm sure you've visited the Lucky Break from time to time while you've been here in Wolf Creek."

"Are you askin' or tellin'?"

"I'm asking, I suppose."

"Then I've been there," Jake said with a nod. "I like it here a mite better."

"It warms my merchant's heart to hear that," Ira said. "But when you were in the Lucky Break, did you notice the house gambler who works for Mayor Henry? I believe he goes by the name Samuel Jones."

"I've seen him." Jake's eyes narrowed slightly. "You say he goes by the name of Jones. Does that mean his real name is something else?"

"Honestly, I don't know, although it seems likely. What I do know is that this morning Jones shot and killed a man in a duel."

Jake nodded slowly. "Heard something about that, too, but I didn't pay it much mind."

"Perhaps you should reconsider and think about it. The man Jones killed had been searching for him. Searching for quite a while, if I had to guess. I spoke to the man. His name was Valentine Hébert. From New Orleans, judging by his accent."

106

Jake regarded him silently for a moment, then said, "This is interestin' as all hell, Mister Breedlove, but I reckon I'd appreciate it if you'd come to the point."

"Of course. Hébert was a hired man. I know one when I see and talk to one. He was working for someone who wants Samuel Jones—or whatever his name really is—dead. Although I would say that it's likely Hébert had a bit of a personal grudge against Jones as well. But what's important is that someone has enough money to pay Hébert to look for Jones and try to kill him."

Jake nodded again. "Which means there's a good chance Jones has got a bounty on his head. I could look into that, try to find out just how much he's worth."

"Or you could just kill him first and then figure it out," Ira suggested.

"I could," Jake said, "but that's not the way I do things."

"Just a suggestion," Ira replied with a shrug.

Jake frowned in thought and rubbed his chin. "I'll see what I can do," he said after a moment. "Maybe send a few telegrams and try to find out something about Mister Samuel Jones and that fella he killed."

Ira spread his hands and said, "However you want to proceed is fine with me. I've done my part."

Jake grunted. "I'd ask why you want me to go after Jones, but I reckon I can make a pretty good guess. You want to get back at his boss for something." The bounty hunter turned to leave but paused in the doorway and looked back at Ira. "Sooner or later, people in this town are gonna have to take sides in a whole new war, ain't they?"

Ira pursed his lips and said, "That's possible, Jake. I'd say that it's very possible indeed."

CHAPTER FIVE

Marshal Gardner hadn't intended to return to his office quite so soon that afternoon. But then he remembered Rupe in the back room, hopefully sleeping off whatever fumes were left of the previous night's toot—unless he'd already wandered off for another poke at the liquor windmill.

Gardner clunked on into his office and hung on the door a moment. "Rupe? You still here?"

He waited a second, heard nothing, then closed the door and dropped his hat on the desktop. He laced his fingers through his hair and sighed. A grunt sounded from the back room. Gardner smiled.

The lawman walked over and leaned against the doorframe. The skinny one-armed drunk lay on his back, eyes closed, his tongue, no doubt feeling dry and wooden, ran slowly inside his mouth, smacking his lips, then he groaned again.

"I figure you might want to get on out of here, maybe get a bite and a beer. What do you say, Rupe?" Sam knew he had Rupe at the word "beer," but he pulled a straight face.

The drunk laid his right hand on the edge of the cot, grunted his way upright, and planted feet to the floor.

"Rupe, if you don't mind me saying, you've looked better."

Rupe rasped his hand across the back of his neck, shook his head. "Yep, I reckon I've been prettier, but it's been a long time since." He offered a weary smile to the marshal.

No matter how many times he hauled the skinny man's backside out of the gutter, Gardner was always amazed at Rupe's capacity for good humor. He could be shaking in the throes of a hard hangover, but he'd still manage a bleary-eyed grin.

"If there was any way I could drag that hangover out of you, why I guess I'd do it, Rupe."

"You had the power to do that, marshal, there's a whole lot of folks in this town who'd pay you for the cure on a daily basis. Nah, I asked for it, I reckon I deserve it. I could sure take you up on that offer of a beer, marshal."

"If you recall, it wasn't only for a beer. Food, too."

Rupe smiled, his eyes closed, his head bobbing almost between his knees. "So that must mean you're still looking for answers to your killing."

"Yep. It's what I do."

"That and a whole passel of other things."

"What do you mean by that?"

"Nothing to get your dander up over, just angling for a joke and not finding a fish."

"For a one-armed drunk, you are a curious man, Rupe."

"You mean you find me a curiosity."

"That's what I said. Now gain your feet and we'll get to it. I have worked up a powerful hunger."

"Okay, okay." Rupe straightened up, his hand visoring his eyes against the day.

A few minutes later found the pair headed along the dirt track between buildings. The afternoon was another warm one and the marshal hung a step or two to the side of his gamey friend. If Rupe noticed he didn't say anything,

"I don't suppose you'd consider stopping off for a bath, Rupe?"

Rupe stopped and sighed. All around him the wilted denizens of Dogleg ambled along. "I can't abide a bath without a shave and haircut first. So I reckon I'll just wait."

Marshal Gardner brightened and laid a hand on his friend's shoulder. "As it happens, I see that Hix has an empty seat in there. What do you say to that?"

"I say I still don't have any money, Sam." Rupe walked on. Sam stood still. Soon enough Rupe stopped, too. "You're going to hold that promised beer just out of reach, aren't you?"

"Yep."

Rupe sighed and turned back toward the barber shop. "Let's get it over with, then."

A few minutes later he was in the chair, much to Hix's dismay. Then the barber slapped Rupe on the head.

"What in the Kee-rist are you doin', Hix?" Tingley spun in the barber chair, tried to free himself of the wrap the barber had draped on him, but only succeeded in further knotting himself in it.

The barber had jumped back out of reach. This sort of reaction from his customers wasn't anything new. In fact, it happened more than he cared to admit.

"I saw a bug of some sort on your head. Figured I'd swat it off for you."

Tingley eyed the barber and rubbed his balding pate with his right hand. "Well I wish to hell you'd ease off such behavior." He slowly turned back around in the seat.

"Or at least warn a body before you commence to rapping him on the bean."

The two men eyed each other in the mirror.

Hix nodded. "I hear you, Rupe." But he knew that as soon as he saw another louse crawling on someone's head, there would be nothing for it but he'd have to swat at it. Such things were the one major misgiving he had with his pursuit of the tonsorial arts. He sighed and did his best to hurry along with the drunk's trim.

For his part, Marshal Gardner had been content to sit back and watch the proceedings with a half-grin, idly playing with the handle of his new walking stick.

Later, after the haircut and shave, and the last of three plates of food at Ma's Café—one for the marshal, two for Rupe, plus a second helping of rum-spiced cobbler—Rupe shook his head once again.

"Marshal, I hate to repay your kindness with silence, but I just can't seem to think of a thing that might help you in tracking down whoever it was who shot that man."

Gardner leaned over his empty plate. "You recall why you went out there?"

"Most likely because I was out of money and out of drink. They seem to go hand in hand, for some odd reason. I guess they're sweet on each other." Then he paused. "You know, I seem to recollect something about that new whiskey peddler. Yes, that's right—he left and I figured he was headed to Asa's, so I followed."

"The whiskey peddler."

"Yep. Thought I might hit him up for a sample or two. Those fellas will sometimes get weary of lugging all that stock around. You got to catch 'em at the right time, though."

"And did it work?"

"Naw, I never made it past the alley."

"Hmm." The marshal nibbled the end of his moustache. "Okay, Rupe." He leaned back and slid a couple of coins across the table. "Why don't you head to Breedlove's house of vice, see how a cool beer goes down? I expect he'll need someone to tidy the place before the evening rush." He slapped the table and stood.

"You're not going?"

"Nope, too much to do." Got to see a man about whiskey, thought Gardner. He paused and in a lower voice said, "Take her easy and keep your head low, you hear? I'll see you later."

Rupe nodded, palmed the coins, and licked his lips. He followed the marshal out the door.

* * *

A rare lance of afternoon light reached through fly-specked glass of the top half of a window just beyond the upright piano. Motes drifted through and were gone from sight again. Rupe stilled his broom and watched as the thick-waisted girl stood with her back to the room.

She wasn't particularly tall, nor even very pretty, but at that moment, with her face to the light, her eyes closed and one hand holding her hair up off her neck, she was the prettiest thing Rupe had seen in a long time. She stood in the bold light like a cat might lie in the sun, feeling that warmth, maybe the only time she'd feel that good all day.

The girl brought to mind others Rupe had known. Lord, but it had been a long time since he'd dallied with a woman, sober, in daylight on clean white bedding. He'd give a lot now if he could spend time with a woman again.

And then the girl let out her breath, dropped her hair, and with it, her shoulders sagged. And as she turned back toward the dim room, Rupe saw the dark-circled eyes, the hard-line mouth, skin showing through the pucker of a missing button, the only boots she owned, beyond cobbling.

How those girls survived as long as they did was a source of puzzlement to him. Shouldn't be, though, he lived a similar thready existence himself. She caught his eye and stared him down hard until he looked away, back to his broom. As it should be—after all, he could only imagine what she saw when she'd looked at him.

"How old are you, anyway, Rupe?"

Rupe's head snapped upright, looked around.

Ira Breedlove was staring at him, a cigar protruding from his pooched lips.

Rupe rubbed a sleeve across his forehead then leaned on the broom like a crutch. "Just how old do you think I am, Mister Breedlove?"

The bar owner squinted at Rupe through a veil of cigar smoke. "Anyone ever tell you it's not polite to answer a question with a question, Rupe?"

The thin drunk smiled and resumed sweeping. "Seems like we're both doing that now."

Breedlove balled up a bar rag and threw it at something behind the counter. Whatever it hit rattled, glass on glass. "I wish to hell you had two arms. Get me twice the amount of work for the same money."

Rupe felt his face heat up. He wanted to give it right back to him, but didn't dare. There were few enough places for him to earn money as it was, no sense soiling this one for himself. He kept silent and retrieved the last of the brass cuspidors. It was half filled with last night's spittle. Rupe carried it with care to the back door.

Behind him he heard Breedlove sigh. "Never let it be said I don't give a damn about my employees."

Rupe heard him, but it was guff. The only thing Ira Breedlove was concerned with was making money. *And so am I*, thought Rupe. *I am not really his employee, anyway. I am what that man had called me before the accident—before I hired on as part of that freighting outfit. An independent contractor. As long as I am paid, I will do what is asked of me. And some day I won't take such insults.*

But he knew he was fooling himself, and always would. Every time he swallowed down another insult, it got easier to swallow the next, and the next. And harder to get his back up. He wasn't even sure he knew how to get good and angry any more.

* * *

It had been a long time since Rupe had reached into a pocket and found money. It usually went from his hand to the bartop. He almost never used the trouser pocket on his left side because that was the side where his arm was missing from the elbow down. Too hard to reach into with his right hand. But when he had dumped out the spittoon, he'd leaned against the edge of that broken table stacked out back and he'd felt something in that pocket.

Investigation, after a few seconds of odd wrangling with his right hand, revealed just shy of three dollars in coins. He gave quick thought as to how it might have ended up in there and figured he'd put it there the previous night, before he'd gone outside to—do what? Somehow that had seemed important.

But he'd found the money an hour earlier, before the bar filled up. Since then, he'd taken that money and put it to good use.

114

"Mack, give me another, will you? I am feeling particularly flush tonight."

The bartender eyed Rupe, who smiled and placed a coin on the bartop as though he were revealing a small but intriguing curiosity no one had ever witnessed before. "As you see, I can pay."

"Wonder of wonders," said Mack and poured Rupe two tight fingers' worth. Rupe didn't even try to hide his dissatisfaction with the man's lack of generosity. "And here I thought we were friends, Mack."

"We are. If I couldn't stand the way you smell—and I can't—I'd leave the bottle."

Rupe licked his lips as he stared at the glass. "I don't know quite what to say to that, but I'll choose it as a compliment. Now, to the matter at hand." He hoisted his glass.

Two drinks later and he'd gotten himself to the point where he felt that warm, fuzzy tingle and his eyesight lost the sharp edges from the previous night's hangover. Then Rupe slowed his drinking. Patrons jostled and elbowed for space at the bar. As the evening ripened, even the cloud of stale sweat around Rupe didn't keep drinking folks from crowding in close. He didn't mind. Some of them even stayed put.

If he wasn't mistaken, one of them was that drummer from the other night, the one with a satchel full of whiskey. It seemed to Rupe he'd been in this same situation the night before, only this time he hoped it might work out better. He giggled out loud.

"What's so funny, drunk?"

The thick-faced man who'd said it had repeated himself, and it was then Rupe thought maybe he'd been talking to him. The finger poke to his shoulder convinced him he was right. Rupe looked at the man. The bar was busy enough that the man stood bare inches from him, and he wore a serious look.

It took Rupe longer than he expected to focus, so he figured that once again he was drunker than he had guessed. "Laugh all you want, but I'll have you know I am a good friend to the marshal."

Rupe was pleased to note that a couple people close by had stopped their chatter and now regarded him in the mirror. He wasted no time in plowing ahead. In his long experience, you get someone hung up on a story you're telling, and you drag it out a bit, it usually is good for a drink or three—depending on the story, of course. But what did he have to offer? Ahh, the shooting would do.

Rupe cleared his throat. "I am what they call a key witness to the events of just last night. In fact, I am the only witness, except for the killer and the dead man. One of them ain't talking and the other one ain't talking—*yet*." Rupe winked, then brayed a little too much at his own joke.

He locked eyes with the whiskey peddler once in the mirror—he'd be the one to impress, a stranger with a poke full of whiskey—but the man looked to be moving, crowded out by the usual faces.

"Then by all means, tell us. Who did the shooting, sir?"

Rupe focused on the source of this new voice and found himself right beside the whiskey peddler—he'd elbowed his way to the bar.

"Well," said Rupe, trying his best not to shrink under the crowd's stares. "I never did see the man's face. But now that I come to think on it, maybe I did see just the back of him—yes, I feel sure I could place him if I had the time."

He scanned the few faces still looking at him, hoping one might have that glint of pity he'd been successful in the past at turning into a drink.

"So," said the smiling salesman. "You're saying the only witness the marshal has is a drunk who doesn't remember a thing, didn't see a thing, and was probably passed out in the alley long before, and after, it all happened."

The peddler looked at his new friends, at the dark-haired girl Rupe had watched earlier, and they all laughed with him, loud, roaring laughter that Rupe should have been used to. But something inside him shriveled even smaller.

"Rupe."

He looked up. The peddler was gone—someone else had said his name. It was Mack.

"Being face-down in the alley, the only thing you'd stand a chance of recognizing is the man's feet!" The comment was met with a burst of louder laughter that crowded out the piano and stray shouts from the other patrons.

Rupe stared down into the empty glass before him, stared with longing at the back bar with the filled bottles like little liquid angels, then shifted his gaze to the laughers. They'd all turned to their own talk, Rupe already a forgotten thing.

Time to call it a night, well before he wanted to—he still had room for a few more drinks, but that didn't look likely. Besides, he had the low gut-aching burn that told him he should have peed long hours before, and an empty pocket with no more glorious coins to buy an evening of forgetting. He threaded his way through the crowd toward the front door and headed left to the alley. No need to find the outhouse when a shadow would do.

* * *

Marshal Gardner had tried his best all day to rattle Rupe's fuzzy mind, but damn if he couldn't get the soak to recall much, other than that the whiskey peddler had left before him. So the marshal had tried to track the man down all afternoon. There couldn't be too many more places the drummer could be holed up.

The night was still young—for Rupe, anyway. Maybe that and the fact that he didn't have any money of his own might have slowed up his drinking. The marshal figured he might catch him at the Wolf's Den. Maybe the damned drummer would be there, too.

Gardner stood just inside the Den's door, waiting as he always did without seeming to appear to take much interest, but secretly enjoying the way the voices drizzled lower and the piano seemed to dim when people finally saw him there. He touched brim to a couple of the ladies, then made his way to the bar. The din picked up again as he entered.

"Excuse me, yep, thanks." He also liked not having to elbow his way in to reach the bar. The drinkers parted when they saw him nearby. "Mack," he nodded to the bartender and waited for the man to make his way down to his end of the bar.

"What can I get for you, Marshal?"

"Sadly, I'm not here for a drink. I'm looking for Rupe."

The big man nodded toward the front door. "You must have walked right by the little soak, Marshal. He wobbled on out of here not a minute ago, maybe less. He always heads off to the alley." He nodded to his left. "He was in here flapping his gums about that killing. Claims he's your only witness. Provided us with quite a show, he did."

"That damn fool." The marshal shook his head, then thought maybe that meant Rupe had remembered something useful. He looked over his shoulder, then turned back. "Hey, Mack, that new whiskey peddler been in here?"

"Yep," the bartender nodded, retrieved an empty mug from the bartop. "He was in here a while ago, too. I don't see him now, though."

"This is not my best day," muttered Gardner. "Thanks, Mack. I'll—"

The distinctive clap of close-by pistol shots, one, then another hot on its heels, sliced through the noisy room and killed all sound. Marshal Gardner had already shucked his sidearm and stiff-legged it to the door, then bent low and peered out the frame. He couldn't see any smoke hanging in the air. He hoped Croy or O'Connor would have heard it, too, and come running.

"Mack! You keep everybody in here don't let anyone leave. I'll be back."

"But Marshal, I can't—"

"Do it, damn you, or you'll answer to me." With that, Gardner skinned low out the left side of the door and hugged the face of the building. "Rupe!" He whispered loud enough for anyone out there to hear him, but he had to know if that big-mouthed drunk was still alive.

"Rupe, it's Sam. If you're alive, let me know. Rupe?"

"Hell yes, I'm alive. No thanks to anybody but me and my lightning reflexes!"

The knot in Gardner's gut loosened. "You hit?"

"Yes, I'm bleedin' somethin' fierce."

The knot clenched tighter and Gardner drew closer to the alley. "Where are you, Rupe? I think whoever shot is gone now." He didn't know that at all, but he had to get to Rupe. And there was no moonlight to be had tonight. He reached for a lucifer, but his boot caught something soft.

"Ouch, hell, Sam. I am shot to pieces and you commence to kicking me? What sort of a lawdog are you, anyway, booting a man when he's down."

He bent low over the drunk. "You only get foul tempered when you're scared, Rupe, so I guess you're good and scared. Am I right?"

"Damn straight I'm scared." Rupe struggled to sit up. "Some fool shot me. Got me bad in the head I think."

Gardner risked a match, thumbed it alight and in the initial flare, saw that Rupe hadn't lied, his face was half covered with blood. But the thin man was sitting up and had an ornery glint in his eye, a good sign. "Lean forward, Rupe, lemme take a look."

"Watch that damn match. I ain't a roasting chicken just yet."

"This doesn't look like a bullet wound, Rupe. You got yourself a cut."

He lit another match, flashed it in front of the stacked wooden crates just behind him. Sure enough a few had been knocked over. "Rupe, I bet you hit your head—I don't think you were shot."

"I know when I've been shot, dammit. My head's all sticky."

Gardner wrinkled his nose at Rupe's whiskey breath as it clouded up at him. "Well, we'll see. I have to get you out of here. You injured anywhere else?"

"I don't know yet. I'm alive, anyway."

By then, despite his warning, a number of people from the bar and street had crowded around, enough so that Gardner felt safe to walk Rupe back inside. Where in the hell were his deputies? Could be anywhere, Wolf Creek was a bigger place than just Dogleg City. "Let's go on inside, see if you're okay."

"Naw, if it's all the same to you. I'd just as soon get away from here. I hate to say it, but I think maybe it's time to go sober for a spell. Least until we find out who's after me."

Sam, still scanning left and right, offered Rupe a hand, and tried to sound casual. "Who's this 'we', Rupe? You got a mouse in your pocket?"

"Well, no. But I ain't about to let somebody take shots at me and get away with it."

"I'd say they sure as hell did get away with it. And besides, you're no use to anyone in your condition." He hauled the thin man to his feet, aware once again of what a fragile creature Rupe really was. Held together by spit and booze—and something more, too, a backbone of wire and nerve.

"Mack." Gardner waited for the bartender to appear on the porch. "Mack, do me a favor and send someone to fetch my deputies. When they get here, tell O'Connor to stay here and send Croy to the jail."

"Will do, marshal."

He did his best to hurry Rupe to the jailhouse despite his own limp, peering left and right, flinching at every cough from the shadows and scratching and scurrying from a rogue cat.

"Why would anyone want to take a shot at me, Sam?" Rupe sounded a lot less hot-headed than he had a few moments before in the alley.

"Mack said you'd been in the bar, yammering about how you'd been the only witness to the shooting. Seems to me there's your reason, right there."

Rupe groaned, though out of dismal realization of his foolishness or out of pain, Gardner couldn't tell. "Hang on, Rupe. We're almost to the jail."

After he toed open the door and shoved Rupe inside, he let out his breath, shuttered the front windows, and lit an oil lamp. "Let's take a look at that fool head of yours."

* * *

Gardner checked Rupe over and found that the blood on his face had come from a cut on his head where he must have fallen. Gardner dabbed it with water and wrapped the drunk's head with gauze. The effect of the swaddling made the marshal laugh, but Rupe didn't seem to care. He looked more miserable than ever.

"I don't suppose any of this knocked loose some scrap of memory that I might find useful?"

"Well, now, let's see...." Rupe thrust his whiskered chin outward, eyes narrowed. "You know how things can look different, depending on where you're at?"

The marshal squinted one eye shut, trying his best to figure out just what sort of logic trail his pickled friend was following. But all the squinting in the world didn't help. "No—no, Rupe, I can't say as I do."

Rupe sighed, then closed his eyes. In the oil lamp's honeyed glow, his eyelids looked thin, like old parchment, as if sunlight might burn right through them. A nerve at the corner of Rupe's left eye jounced in counterpoint to the fluttering lids.

"No, I don't expect it's anything you'd know. I ..." Rupe opened his eyes again and, as impossible as it seemed, Tingley looked even older and more drawn to the marshal.

"Rupe, just what are you getting at?" Gardner rattled tepid coffee into a chipped tin cup.

"From the floor, marshal. Down low. I was thinking how things look changed when you're on the ground. Different perspectives, as they say."

"Rupe, you confound me. One minute you're singing or crying, according to the level of booze in your gullet, the next you're moping around town all hangdog and dribbling out two-dollar words like you had some education backing you up."

It occurred to the marshal he might just be the case. Just what did he know about Rupe, anyhow? Only what he'd told him when he'd showed up in town a few years before, afoot, drunk, and half-dead from the spring winds that had all but peeled the skin off the skinny drink of water.

"Ah, it ain't no use, Sam."

He looked more to the marshal like an injured bird that couldn't fend for itself, off-balance and trying to make up for it by leaning too far one way, the man's head wobbling in the other direction. The wet eyes and trembling lip, the shot nerves all told Marshal Gardner his drunken friend couldn't be long for this world. Then again, he'd seen such characters outlive healthy, working folk. Unfair or not, the Lord does protect a drunk, he thought.

Gardner slid open a bottom drawer on the desk and tossed a boot bottle to Rupe. It arced in the air, halfway to the seated man, when the marshal winced—he'd just thrown a glass bottle to a one-armed man, a shaking, drunken one-armed man, at that. But bird-thin Rupe surprised him. That one good wing fluttered up, snatched and pulled in the bottle, hugging it to his belly. "What's this for?"

"Ain't much left, but I figure it'll even you out. We have some talking to do and I can't have you spending the entire time licking your lips and thinking about how fast you can get to the nearest bar. I need you to focus on what we're saying. Call that gargle my payment on a conversation."

Rupe wasted no time in upending the bottle. His throat worked as if he'd been in the desert for days without water. He stopped with a few swallows left, ran his hand across his lips, then said, "I've spent a goodly portion of my time these last few years on my belly, marshal. Mostly because I can't for the life of me figure out how to get back up."

"I've never pried, Rupe, you know that. But if there's ever something you need to talk about, well, I'm as good a listener as a bottle—and a whole lot less costly and troublesome."

"Not nearly so fun, though." Rupe snorted a quick laugh.

"Well thanks all to hell—I think."

But Rupe's face grew serious. "Breedlove said something earlier that got me thinking. You know, Sam, how one thing will lead to another in your mind. Before you know it, you've gone so far from where you began, you got no idea where you are or how you got there?"

"That's happened to me a time or two—take this conversation, for example. I haven't got a clue as to what you're on about."

"Okay, okay. Breedlove, he asked me how old I was. We played slap-and-tickle with that for a minute, but it got me to thinking back to when I was a freighter. I told you about that." Rupe nodded at the marshal.

Gardner returned the gesture, curious to know here this was going.

"Had my own rig, an old ore wagon I got for a song, fixed her up, painted her blue, and got me a three-yoke team. God, but I loved them boys. Ain't nothing we couldn't haul. I'd hire out for pretty near any job, I was that sure of 'em ."

"Good paying work, hauling freight," said Gardner.

"You bet it was. And it was honest work, I tell you. I had two arms then, and money in my pocket. And for a time, I had me the closest I'll ever come to a son. Boy I called Davey." He looked at the marshal with a shine in his eyes and a faint smile on his face. "I never knew his right name, and if he did, he never told me. Never did speak. He wasn't but seven or eight when I come up on him. There was a burned-out wagon, three dead bodies. It was his ma and pa and sister, I reckon, from what I could make of the scene. Sioux, I'd guess. They laid them low, must have stolen their horses, put flame to everything else."

"How'd the boy live through it?"

"Hid himself in a gully, but he saw the whole thing. He was a tough character, though. It was most likely a week since it had happened that I come along. Did my best to bury them proper. I was in the midst of it when that kid jumped right on my back! Thought I had a lion on me. I got him calmed down in the end." Rupe smiled to himself at the memory.

Gardner sipped the cold coffee and said, "What happened to him? You never mentioned having a boy."

"I had him a couple of years. I'd grown right fond of him, never could figure out who his people were, nor where they had come from, where they were headed. So I just took him on as my own. He was tough, by God. I expect he would have taken over the business, but them damned Sioux. Murdering sons-of-bitches...."

The marshal nodded, but said nothing. He'd never heard this story before, but he'd heard plenty of similar stories, and he could guess what was coming.

"They got us one day when we were too far from anywhere to make a run for it. Must have been five or six of them. First thing I knew of it I saw arrows sticking out of my oxens' backs. They never had time to do more than tear at the traces before those Indians come down at us out of the hill to our right, like screaming birds. I was reaching for the shotgun but damn, I had no time. One of them rode right up, hit me on the back of the head with what, I never saw. It was enough of a blow to drop me from the wagon. Then I got an arrow in the arm, pinned me to the ground just as neat as you please." He wagged his stumped arm, the ragged shirt sleeve flapped at his side.

"I come around in time to see Davey had been laid right, arrows and cuts all over him, but he was a fighter. Kicking and biting and grabbing, just like a lion. I tell you, Sam, that kid was a tough one."

Gardner was about to speak, but Rupe continued. "One of them bastards, a fat one, I remember—had no shirt and he was built like a sloppy woman—that bastard knelt hard right on the boy's chest."

Rupe's voice cracked, he closed his eyes and ran his hand under his nose. His voice grew husky, deeper. "Took Davey's topknot. But it was a messy affair. I suspect that damned Indian's blade was dull. The boy wasn't yet dead, still bleeding out, and the blood from his head bubbled and washed down his face, thick like molasses. I can still smell it—hot and raw like something a body shouldn't ever have to smell. Oh, God, and his eyes fluttered open and he stared right at me. Give me a look."

He looked at the marshal, his eyes wet. "Do you know, that look on his young face wasn't one of blame. No sir, it was one of forgiveness. And I ain't telling a windy, because forgiveness is the last thing I want or deserve. But that boy, in his last seconds of life, he was more man than I have ever been, or will ever be."

His bandaged head slumped back down between the points of his shoulders, and it was a long minute before the marshal realized the pathetic one-armed drunk was sobbing. A tear ran off Rupe's thin nose, hit the wood floor. "I couldn't move. I thought I was dying, when that savage hit my head I couldn't feel anything. I wish to hell I had died then, I tell you. They didn't even see fit to scalp me. Just left me alive, damn their eyes."

"It ain't too late, Rupe. You could do that boy proud yet—"

Faster than Gardner had ever seen the man move, Rupe jumped to his feet and pointed a long, trembling finger at him. "No sir, don't you dare! You may have picked me up off my face more times than I deserve, might have gotten me paying work that a one-armed man ought not have, might have bought me more meals than a body such as me has a right to eat, might have bought me this haircut and shave, but that don't never give you nor anybody else the right to tell me what I should be doing where that boy's memory is concerned."

In a lowered, shaking voice he said, "I should never have talked of it." He made for the jailhouse door, then stopped and made his way to the back room. The marshal heard him lie down on the bunk.

Sam Gardner stayed in his chair for a long time, staring at that spot on the floor long after Rupe's tear had dried.

* * *

Gardner had been considering making another pot of coffee—it was going to be a long night—when from the back room he heard—not Rupe's snores, as he expected—but the sound of the man getting up off the bunk. Then Rupe appeared in the doorway.

"Can't sleep?"

"Brogans."

"What?"

"Remember how I said how things look different from the ground, how I spent so much time down there it seems natural somehow?"

"Yeah, sure. What of it?"

Rupe rubbed his hand along his cheek, wincing as his fingertips grazed the bandage looped under his chin. "I told you I didn't really see what happened last night, not even the man's back. But I did see something."

Gardner dropped his boots to the floor and leaned forward, eyes narrowed. "Yeah?"

Rupe nodded, walked to the stove, held out his hand, though the stove was long cold. "I wasn't lying then, I just couldn't recall much. But I have, you see. Now I have." He turned to face Gardner, a smile tugging at his mouth. "Brogans."

"You already said that, Rupe."

"Yeah, but I'm telling you I think the shooter wore brogans. Hell, I'd swear to it."

Gardner stood, the wooden chair stuttering on the floor. "Rupe, are you damn sure? Do you know what you're saying?"

"Yeah, I know, not a whole lot of people wear brogans, but this fella did."

Gardner fingered his moustache. "You sure it's a man, then?"

"Course I'm sure. I ain't never been so drunk I can't tell the difference betwixt a jack and a jenny."

"You know how many men wear brogans in this town, Rupe."

"You askin' or tellin', Sam?" Rupe didn't even turn around as he said it, just headed into the back room. Presently, Rupe said, "I know of one man who wears brogans in this town. And now I wish I hadn't remembered a damn thing. And Sam?"

"Yeah, Rupe."

"What I talked of before...."

"It's between us, Rupe. Nobody else."

"Appreciate it, Sam."

There was quiet for a moment, then Gardner heard Rupe lay down again and soon, the steady, heavy breaths of a man dropping like a stone into a deep sleep.

Gardner sighed and stoked the near-dead coals in the stove. He envied Rupe. There wouldn't be any sleep for him or his deputies this night, so he'd better make coffee and hope Croy or O'Connor made it back before too long. They had people to talk to, things to look at, work to do.

The knot in his gut eased a bit. He tried to concentrate on the killing, but his mind fixed on Rupe's young tortured boy, Davey, staring at Rupe as he died.

* * *

"Aw, hell no...." Gardner pushed himself back up to his knees and slapped his palms on his legs.

"What?" Deputy Croy paused, squinting in the morning sun at the mouth of the alley. His hand rested on a wobbling stack of barrel staves behind which he was definitely not finding sign of brogans. "Marshal, I hope that means you found something, because I'm just wasting my time back here."

Gardner jerked his chin toward the dirt before him.

Croy pushed his hat back and leaned in. He kept his voice low. "They made by brogans, you think?"

"Yep."

"Some boots might make the same prints as brogans, though."

"True, but there's more. That one there? What do you see?"

Croy bent lower, much the same as Gardner had.

"Hey, you two...." Ira Breedlove leaned on the paint-faded post at the corner of the porch, half smiling. "Little early to be face-down in the dirt, even for you all."

The lawmen both looked up at him. "Mind your own, Breedlove," said Gardner, then directed his attention back to the tracks before them.

Straightening up as if he'd been slapped, Breedlove looked around to see if anyone had heard the exchange. Then he muttered "ungrateful bastard," and headed back inside.

"It's that curvy bit there you're pointing at, right?"

"Yep," said Gardner, leaning in again. "That's Rattlesnake Jake's mark. Likes to wear his brogans and likes everyone to know he's a hard case."

Croy kept staring at the mark. "From what I've seen and heard, he looks to be one."

"In my experience, Quint, any man who has to go out of his way to prove he's mean and ornery isn't really much of either."

The men stood and looked down the nearly empty street.

"There are always exceptions," said Croy.

"Yep. I reckon we'll find out presently if Jake's one or not." Marshal Gardner started walking. "First, you can buy me a cup of coffee."

Deputy Croy shook his head and followed the marshal.

INTERLUDE

Samuel Jones liked to take his breakfast at Isabella's Restaurant. Most folks in town who could afford to eat away from home preferred Ma's Café, or Joe's Whistle-stop up by the depot—they were less pricey, and served up more familiar fare. Jones, though, could afford to splurge, and Isabella's was worth splurging on—especially to him. Samuel Jones might have been a wayward cardsharp, but he had spent most of his life in New Orleans as Philippe Beaumont.

Antonio Isabella was a cheerful Italian in his early fifties. As a young sailor he had fallen in love with New Orleans, and married a girl from there—they now had a houseful of kids, and a kitchen whose savory aromas were a mix of Italian, Spanish, and French. The smells of the Crescent City, in other words. And whichever name he used, breakfast was not breakfast to the gambler unless it included andouille sausage.

It was surprising, and a little unnerving, how many people with New Orleans connections lived in Wolf Creek. There were the Isabellas, Spike Sweeney the blacksmith, and of course Jones himself. Fortunately, the other former New Orleans dwellers had not moved in the same circles as Jones, and thus had not recognized him. It was safe, therefore, for him to occasionally get a taste of home without answering any questions about his own past life. People in Wolf Creek didn't ask questions, anyhow. Most of them had their own secrets to keep.

His reverie—and his meal—were interrupted by an unexpected visitor. A man in a cheap, rumpled suit sat across from Jones. He was about forty-five years old, balding, and carried a weathered carpetbag. After a moment Jones placed him—it was the new whiskey peddler, the one who'd replaced Lester Weatherby after the recent Kiowa incident.

"We haven't officially met, sir," the drummer said. "My name is Malchius Offerman."

Jones nodded. "Whiskey peddler."

"Yes indeed."

"It's a mite early for me, Mister Offerman."

The drummer smiled, but it was a cold smile. "I'm not here in that capacity, Mister Jones. And yes, I know your name, even though we haven't met—you were the talk of the town last night, after that duel."

Jones popped the last bite of sausage into his mouth. "Which is better than being the talk of the town because one is dead," he said, then polished off his eggs.

"No doubt, Mister Jones, no doubt. And I've asked around—Valentine Hébert wasn't the first man you've killed in Wolf Creek. You've outdrawn a couple of people who tried to protest your poker skills with bullets."

Samuel Jones put down his coffee cup, and his eyes narrowed. "I recall now," he said, "that the marshal was asking after you at the Lucky Break yesterday evening."

Offerman shrugged. "That's neither here nor there."

Jones leaned forward. "Let me guess, Mister Offerman. My gunplay has impressed you, and you've thought of some angle to use it to attract customers and sell drinks."

The cold smile returned. "Oh, no, Mister Jones," the drummer replied. Then he looked around to make sure no one was sitting nearby, and continued in a soft voice. "I want you to help me kill someone."

Samuel Jones was not often surprised anymore, but this had done it.

"I know, I know," the drummer said, "you are a professional gambler. But I know a gunman when I see one. I've been around enough, believe me. I can pay you very well."

"Keep talking."

"I assume you know the bounty hunter who hangs around this town from time to time, the one they call Rattlesnake Jake?"

"I know him. Not well, but I know him. And I know he didn't get that nickname because he shakes a rattle. He is a very dangerous man."

"I'm well aware of that," Offerman said. "That's why I haven't tried to accomplish this goal by myself— believe me, I would like nothing better, but I wouldn't have a chance. Even trying to bushwhack a man like that by yourself is too risky. That's why I need help. And that's why the marshal couldn't find me last night—I was down in Tent City, trying to recruit some helpers. I got three men, but I need a real professional to seal the deal."

"I see. So you're not really a whiskey drummer at all."

Offerman chuckled. "That's the funny part," he said. "I really am. I've had my eye on this town for awhile, trying to work out the best angle to get at him—and when that blithering coward Weatherby quit, I jumped at the chance to take over his route. It's the perfect cover, because it's not a cover. And I do have a little money, mostly from selling my father's house and hardware store down in Austin when he passed away."

"What business does a whiskey drummer have with a hard-case bounty hunter?" Jones asked.

"That's my affair," Offerman said, and Jones shook his head.

"I'm afraid not," Jones said. "If you're asking me to go up against someone that I know to be a dangerous gunfighter, I want to know what your stake is."

Offerman bit his lip and considered his reply for a moment. "All right, I'll tell you. He murdered my little brother in St. Joe two years ago. He was only my half-brother, and he was an idiot, but I loved him. Clyde robbed a bank in Austin and took to the outlaw trail, but he didn't kill anybody. Someone else in the gang shot the tellers. He didn't deserve to die for it. Clyde's death broke our father's heart, and I believe that's what killed him."

Samuel Jones could read faces, it was his job. Offerman's eyes were equal parts fury and grief. He could tell that the drummer's story was true—at least from his perspective. Although his love for his kid brother was definitely obscuring his objectivity; someone who robs a bank in which a teller gets killed would be guilty of second degree murder in most states whether they pulled the trigger or not. The gambler deemed it unwise to point that out under the circumstances, though. When a man loses a brother, especially a younger one, reason often goes out the window.

Jones nodded his understanding.

"What do I have to do?" he asked.

CHAPTER SIX

"That's him over there in the corner, at the back. But, beggin' your pardon, ma'am, I just have to ask, have you given sufficient thought to seekin' out a bounty hunter to track your husband? You're likely to end up without your money or your husband," Mack, the bartender of the Wolf's Den, said, with a wizened leer as he wiped a wet spot on the polished bar for the fifth time. "Now, for the right price–"

"You let me worry about whether I get my husband back, or not. I'll thank you to mind your own business," the petite lady answered curtly, spinning around and walking away. She had hair black as night and eyes green as emeralds

The bartender, red-faced at being dressed-down by a lady in front of his other customers–all two of them–went back to wiping the same spot for the sixth and seventh times. The lady sashayed over to the table of a man with a face that looked like a well-traveled road, ruts and all. He was shuffling and reshuffling a badly worn deck of cards, bent, cracked, and dirty.

"You the man they call Rattlesnake Jake? The bounty hunter?" she asked.

"Maybe. Who's askin'?"

"I'm Teresa Munder and my husband is missing. I want him back."

Jake recognized the last name. Alexander Munder was a pain in the ass—he made the rounds of every saloon in town about once a week, crying in his beer and everyone else's about what a bitch his wife was. Jake had always figured anyone who had to put up with that whining bastard was justified in treating him like shit.

"Why?" Jake asked.

"Why did he go missing or why do I want him back?"

"Take your pick." The man spread the cards out in front of him then flipped the whole row with the one card still in his hand.

"Well, to start with, I'm unwilling to believe he just up and abandoned me. He's not that kind. And I doubt he's taken up with another woman."

"Why?"

"Because he's a hard-working, honorable man and he wouldn't let himself be caught up on a whim by another pretty face."

"When did he go missing?"

"Two days ago."

Jake grinned. "Hell, that's not even long enough for a good drunk. He's probably sleepin' it off somewhere."

"He is not. Alexander always comes home by dawn— he did not, not dawn yesterday and not dawn today. And he is not, as you say, sleeping it off—I have been to every bar in town and no one has seen him since Monday night. Today is Wednesday, in case you don't keep track."

"What was the last thing he said before he left?"

"He said, 'Damn you woman, I'm a man with needs and…' Oh never mind. It's not important what he said. I want to know how much you need to be paid to find him."

"How much is he worth to you?"

"I have, er, a thou…uh…about five hundred dollars saved up."

"Uh-huh." He reshuffled the deck again, peeling off the top four cards and turning them over. Four aces.

"Well, will you do it?"

"I'll give you some damned good advice. And it won't cost you one red cent."

"What's that?"

"Give it up. When a man like Alexander Munder goes on the scout, it's because he don't want to be found."

"H-how did you know my husband's name?"

"Hell, lady, everybody in Wolf Creek knows Alexander Munder. They all know he's got a beautiful wife whose colder'n an icicle."

"Wha-what did you call me?"

"A beautiful ice queen, that's all. Deny it." He put the aces back in the deck, reshuffled three or four times, then peeled the top four off again. And, once more, turned up four aces.

Tears flooded the lady's eyes as she looked around, obviously embarrassed by what this crude man had said. She started to reply, but instead, dropped into one of the captain's chairs across the table from Rattlesnake. She put her face in her hands and began to sob.

Rattlesnake said nothing. He did, however, continue to do card tricks, repeatedly flipping over aces. After several minutes, with tears still streaming down her face, she fixed a sad gaze on him. Her voice had turned from strong woman to helpless child.

"Please. I need help and don't know who else to turn to. Won't you help me?"

Ever the sucker for a sobbing female, Rattlesnake tossed the deck of cards down on the table, revealing that every card in the deck was an ace, and pushed his chair back, stood, and snapped his suspenders.

"Aw, hell, why not. I could use the money. Up front, of course," he said, as though it were neither a statement nor a question. He cocked his head and raised one eyebrow. He expected a reluctance to let go of five hundred dollars without some guarantee of success. He was surprised by her response.

"Of course," she said, pulling a small, embroidered purse from one of her pockets. She peeled off five one hundred dollar bills and handed them to him. "Do I get a receipt?"

"Me findin' your husband will be all the receipt you'll need. If I don't, then you're just out the money. Findin' a wayward husband is always a gamble."

"That's not a very honorable way to do business if you want people to feel comfortable in the arrangement," she said, having regained her composure and her stiffness.

"Reckon you're right. But them's the terms. Your choice."

She looked at the floor for a moment, twisting a dainty foot left and right. Jake figured his cavalier attitude had turned her off and she would say *forget it, I'll find someone else.* He was surprised by her next words and they had nothing to do with money or rewards or receipts.

"I-I just can't fathom why he'd leave me."

"Because, a man only leaves a beautiful lady if things aren't goin' the way he thinks they should at home. And forgive my boldness, ma'am, but you are a beautiful lady.

139

Or, he leaves for perfectly legitimate reasons and gets himself robbed and killed, or he falls into a ravine and breaks his fool neck. If I find the second reason is what happened to him, do you want his body back, or will some identifiable object do?"

"Bring him back no matter what you find," Mrs. Munder said curtly.

"As you wish," he said. "Oh, one more thing—what color was the horse he rode out on?"

"His favorite, a grey gelding."

He pulled his .36-caliber Colt Navy and checked to make sure he'd remembered to reload after the last time he'd had to use it. He also needed to be certain all the percussion caps were seated properly—they were, so he let it drop back into the holster. He watched the lady walk out the front of the saloon, turn right, and disappear down the boardwalk.

He knew damned well this job was going to be trouble. If he weren't strapped for cash, he'd have ignored her, or possibly tried to get her into bed. She was one damned fine looking lady, not his usual type of overweight whore or saloon queen. But once he came back with the bad news about her husband–and he knew that's what it would be, no matter what–she'd turn her back on him because of her shame in having to seek out a paid piece of pond scum to find the man she thought she loved. She didn't really, though, and he knew it. He could tell by the look in her eyes and the way her lip curled when she said his name. Oh, and those tears, they were phony. She wanted him back so she could slap him down in front of everyone just one last time. Rattlesnake's imagination painted a picture as to what might lie in store for Mr. Alexander Munder if he had to face his wife one more time. The bounty hunter could already hear the explosion and smell the cordite as the man's blood spurted from his chest and he crumpled to the ground. The comely Teresa Munder's plea to the court would go something like *He beat me and called me monstrous names, drove me near to insanity! I had to do it, don't you see? It was him or me.*

Rattlesnake doubted the validity of any such claim, but that didn't mean she wouldn't get away with it. Courts tended to sympathize with grieving widows, whether they were the cause of the poor man's demise or not. Especially a pretty widow who could conjure up a flood of tears on command.

Anyways, it was something to do. Of course, Ira had potentially put him on the scent of a well-paying prize in that gambler from the Lucky Break. Samuel Jones. He seemed like a pretty competent man with a gun, even before this dueling incident, but Jake had never really given him much thought before. If there was a bounty for him, Jake would earn it—but he wasn't going to just call the man out on the off chance it could turn a profit, no matter how bad Ira wanted him to do so. Jake had gone over to the telegraph office as soon as they opened up, and sent out some feelers on Jones. Any more action on that front would have to wait till he got the information he needed.

Jake slid his beat-up, flat-crowned, floppy-brimmed hat off the table, slapped it on his leg—releasing a cloud of dust—pulled it low over his eyes, and went to the door. Teresa Munder must have already ducked into one of the stores down the street and could no longer be seen. *Good*, he thought, *I'd rather she not watch where I intend to start my search.* He sauntered outside, looked around, then slowly made his way around the building, down Fifth Street to the back alleyway, then across to the rear of several clapboard buildings. He planned to follow that route until he was at least a block down before entering the rear of Miss Abby's cathouse. As he prepared to step up on the porch, he noticed a grey gelding in the corral behind the place. He knocked first, then entered. He was greeted by a short, petite lady who was probably still in her twenties but had eyes much older. She was wearing too much make up and penciled-on eyebrows. Miss Abby, herself.

"Well, I'll be damned, if it ain't ol' Rattlesnake Jake. Finally got enough together for a poke?" She gave him a come-hither grin and attempted to take his arm.

"Got the money, Abby, but not the inclination. Leastways not right now. I'm lookin' for someone."

"And just who would that someone be?" She gave him a wink.

"Alexander Munder."

Abby took a step back, swallowing hard and nearly tripping on one of three overstuffed chairs that lined the hallway, where gentlemen could wait their turn at one of her girls. The look on her face suggested she was scared to death. Rattlesnake knew that meant she either knew where Munder was or had seen him recently.

"Wh-why, er, what do you want with him?"

"So, you have seen him?"

"Maybe, maybe not. Can't rightly remember."

"Think on it, Abby, and think real hard." Rattlesnake let his hand drop to the butt of his Colt.

"You been here plenty of times, yourself, and you know how things can get out of hand. Sometimes two fellas are lookin' for the favor of the same girl at the same time. When a man is ready, he don't show a lot of patience. You know that."

"So, what happened when Munder and some other fella had the same hankerin'?"

"A-a big ol' argument, that's what. When tempers flare, uh, weapons show up almost outta nowhere."

"Was Munder armed?"

"I, uh, don't think so," Abby said.

"And–?"

"And the other fella—he was touchy as hell, he sure didn't look like the type—he grabbed Munder by the scruff of the neck and drug him downstairs and around back. The fella had one of them Arkansas toothpicks like you and Ira Breedlove carry and, maybe he took it out when they got out yonder—maybe Mister Munder lunged for him, and, uh, he mighta stuck hisself. I don't know, didn't nobody see, exactly. The damnedest thing is, that other fella never even came back in, after he got so worked up—it's like he was lookin' for an excuse to pick a fight."

"Uh-huh. Was Munder alive when you last saw him?"

"Well, I couldn't rightly tell. His face was turned away from me when they hauled him outta here. He was bleedin' some, though."

"Once more, Abby, was he alive? Don't make me ask again."

Abby's head drooped and her chubby right hand shot to her throat and quickly grasped a silver cross that hung around her neck on a chain. "I'm thinkin' it ain't likely. He was bleedin' from a slit in his throat."

"Did anyone go for the sheriff or the marshal?"

Abby's expression was one of incredulity.

"Are you serious? Why a thing like this could put me out of business. Couldn't risk it."

"What did you do with him?"

Abby shrugged meekly. "Sometimes, when stuff like that happens, we haul 'em down to Tent City and toss 'em in the creek. With rocks in their pockets. You know, to protect our business."

"Who did it, Abby? Who had the pig sticker?"

She looked away and took a step further down the hall. He reached out a grabbed her arm. She muttered, "I-I can't tell you."

"Can't or won't?"

"Don't make no difference. A man is dead and I can't bring him back. No matter who killed him, Alexander Munder ain't of this world, no more. And now, it's time for you to take your leave."

"I'm goin' nowhere until I get the name of the man who killed Munder. Either give him up or expect me to be sittin' right here, makin' sure no horny cowboy makes it past me. I figure you'll be broke in three days. The mayor and the sheriff will still be expecting their cut of your haul each day, and I doubt they'll buy your story of bein' too damned poor to make their payoff all because of a little business downturn."

Abby dropped into the first chair she came to, fanning her red face with her hand. Her eyes were glazed over as she contemplated the threat made to her by the bounty hunter. Rattlesnake turned the first chair around so it would face the doorway. He plopped down, crossed his legs at the ankles, drew his Colt and began to whistle. It was no more than a few minutes before an anxious cowboy blew through the door hollering for Becky. Abby's eyes shot open and her mouth fell open as she heard Rattlesnake's words.

"Sorry, cowboy, Abby's whorehouse is closed for business," Jake said. "Try one of the cribs in back of

Asa's Saloon. They're a little raunchy, but what the hell. When a man just has to have a little—"

"Some new fella, calls hisself Malchius Offerman! He's a whiskey drummer, he just took over Lester Weatherby's route," Abby blurted out as she leaped up from her chair. "Now go, Rattlesnake, so's I can show this fine young man to Becky's room."

Rattlesnake tipped his hat to Abby with a wry grin. "Thank you, ma'am. Most generous."

He grunted to himself as he walked away. Damn peculiar behavior for a whiskey peddler.

* * *

The bounty hunter calmly strolled out the front door this time and turned down Grant Street to return to the Wolf's Den. He was in serious need of a whiskey, or maybe two, and a place to sit. And think. And plan. The task before him presented a considerable risk. The town seemed to be bleeding a lot of late.

He'd no sooner taken up his same old chair at the same old table, the one which everybody in town knew was his and his alone, when Deputy Quint Croy peeked in and entered, crossing quickly to where Jake sat staring at the mound of cards in front of him.

"Jake, the marshal wants to see you. 'You find that scoundrel and fetch him here and right now!' he says to me. So, get your ass outta that chair and come along."

Jake looked at the deputy with a 'go-to-hell' expression, beginning to reorganize his stack of pasteboards.

"Why couldn't he come hisself?"

"Because he's the marshal, that's why, and he don't chase down suspected killers on his own. He sends out his tougher-than-hell deputy, me. So, let's get goin'."

Jake smiled coldly at the deputy. "You sound a lot tougher'n you look, boy."

"Try me and see," Quint replied, and the bounty hunter shrugged.

"What's all this shit about me bein' a 'suspected killer'? Who the hell am I supposed to have killed?"

"Reckon you'll find out soon enough, tough guy. Now get the hell up." Croy let his hand drop to his holstered revolver.

Jake made no move toward his own. Instead, he let out a groan as he struggled to his feet, faking a drunken attempt to regain his balance. In an instant, however, the deputy was staring down the barrel of Jake's Navy Colt and into the narrowed eyes of a man with little patience.

"Now hold on, Jake. I—"

"Yeah, I know, you're just doin' what the marshal sent you to do. And he probably told you that young lawmen need to be especially tough with low types like me. You tell the marshal I'll drop by as soon as I tend to a little business—and it'll be in my own good time. But I'll tell you this, and I'll say it only once, if you ever talk to me like that again, I'll blow your damned head clean off. Now get the hell out of here."

Croy backed slowly up, making certain to keep his hands far away from his hogleg. Perspiration slowly trickled down his cheeks and he swallowed hard as he stared into the steely eyes of a man he knew was capable of carrying out his threat. He had nearly lost his balance a couple of times bumping into chairs on his way to the door, and a look of relief came over him when he could feel the batwings behind him. He spun around and made a beeline for the boardwalk, his cheeks red with embarrassment. He was still retreating when Jake leaned out with a satisfied grin.

The bartender came up and said, "What the hell was all that about?"

"Don't know. But I figure on finding out." With that, Rattlesnake Jake left the saloon.

* * *

Jake was wondering if his conversation with Abby had already gotten back to the marshal, and an assumption had been made that he was somehow involved in Munder's death. He was headed to the marshal's office, for sure, mainly because he didn't intend on getting a visit from more than one deputy. Marshal Gardner liked having several deputies hanging around, both so he could spend most of his time in saloons or with his feet up on his desk. But before Jake got there, he had a couple places he wanted to stop, first. One of those places was the saloon where this Offerman was rumored to hang out. And while he wouldn't recognize the man if he was sitting right next to him, he figured he knew someone who could point him in the right direction: Mayor Dab Henry. Dab's saloon, The Lucky Break, was the starting point for almost anyone looking for information. It was a place that never lacked for loose talk. And loose women. And men with bad attitudes.

Jake stood outside for a brief moment before entering, peering through the front window to get a lay of the land. Always cautious where guns and liquor were the most prevalent commodities, he hadn't lived as long as he had without being careful. Seeing nothing suspicious, he eased through the front door and went straight for the bar.

"Dab here?" he asked Rob Parker, the burly bartender.

"Was, until a few minutes ago."

"So, he left?"

"Ain't that what I just said?" The bartender continued stacking glasses on the back bar in a pyramid shape, keeping his back to the bounty hunter. The man's smartass mouth was going to get him in trouble, someday. Jake had a sudden impulse to make today that day.

Jake drew his Colt and cocked it. He snarled, and his eyes narrowed. Then he said, "Where did he go? And if I hear any more of your lip, jackass, they'll be stackin' those glasses on your coffin."

The bartender got the picture quickly. He finally turned to face his inquisitor.

"I, uh, don't know exactly," Parker said, "but he and that Offerman fella left in kind of a hurry."

That piece of unexpected information hit Jake like a low punch. What connection could there possibly be between a piece of scum like Offerman and Wolf Creek's erstwhile mayor? While Offerman was known to hang around The Lucky Break, Jake had never heard anything to suggest Mayor Henry cavorted with his customers on any kind of regular basis. Then he remembered that Offerman was a whiskey drummer—Dab would hang out with a drummer sure enough, there might be money in it somewhere.

Maybe he shouldn't put off seeing the marshal any longer. Could be there were answers in that unlikely place that need following up on. The bartender hadn't moved an inch, as Jake seemed to take his sweet time chewing on what he'd heard. There was an audible sigh coming from behind the bar as Jake suddenly spun around and headed for the door.

Wolf Creek: Murder in Dogleg City

The marshal's office was at the corner of Fourth and Second Streets, three blocks from The Lucky Break. A short three minutes would have him pushing through Marshal Sam Gardner's office door. The second place he'd wanted to stop by would just have to wait.

When he walked in, Marshal Gardner was reading a newspaper, feet up on his desk. Quint Croy was nowhere to be seen, nor was the other deputy. Gardner looked over the top of his paper, eyeing Jake warily.

"Good to see you could tear yourself away from whatever shady scheme you were cooking up in order to drop by, Jake," Gardner said.

"Yeah, well, your errand boy made it clear you were pretty lathered up about somethin'. So, let's get to it."

"Don't get all tangled up in your spurs, Jake, this is complicated business. And I figure you're right in the middle of it."

"And just what business might that be, Marshal?"

"Murder, Jake. Plain and simple."

"Who was murdered?"

"I figured you'd know, since the evidence is pointed straight your way." The marshal pulled a cigar from his vest pocket, reached for a sulfur from a tin box, pulled one out and dragged it across the desktop. He lit the cigar, leaned back, and blew smoke across the room.

If the marshal was calling him a murderer, why was the bastard taking his own sweet time getting on with it? That's what struck Jake as odd. He'd known Gardner for a couple of years and he seemed to be a no-nonsense lawman, if a tad tight with paying out bounties. But generally a decent sort. That's what made Jake willing to come to Gardner's office of his own accord. It seemed to him that if he were going to be dragged in, accused of a crime for which there must be ample evidence he'd done it, Quint Croy would've already tried to do the dragging, and would've brought plenty of back-up. Since that hadn't happened, Jake figured the marshal was just pulling his line through the water hoping to get a bite.

"Just what evidence are you yakkin' about? Let's get on with details, here, Gardner. I've got things to attend to."

"Fair enough. You likely heard about the body that was found down near the river, back of Asa Pepper's Saloon. A fellow named Laird Jenkins. Ever heard of him?"

"No. What makes you think I might have?"

"We found ourselves some evidence nearby. And like I said, it points directly at you."

"What evidence would that be?"

"Foot prints. The kind those brogans of yours make. You been back of Pepper's place recently?"

"Hell, no! I wouldn't frequent that joint if you paid me. Pepper's the kind of slime I steer clear of. And what makes you think I'm the only soul in town that wears brogans?"

Gardner thought about that for a minute, blowing the most inept smoke rings Jake had ever seen. He was tempted to ask for a cigar of his own just to show the marshal how it was done. But he didn't. Instead, he sat quietly, studying the lawman, and wondering who this Laird fellow was and why anyone thought Jake would want to kill him.

Jake was shaken from his woolgathering when Gardner said, "You're not. But you are the only one who pounds an S-shaped nail into his soles, to look like a snake. At least, so far as I know, you are. But I had to be sure. So I went to the cobbler and asked him. Know what I found out?"

"No. But I'll bet you're fixin' to tell me."

"I am. He told me he sells ten to twelve pairs every year to all sorts of folks. But you *are* in fact the only one who asks for that special mark. In fact, he told me to tell you he's anxious to order your next pair because he figures the ones you've worn for two years are surely worn down to nothing. So that got me to thinking."

"I like a man who thinks, at least on occasion. Just what were you thinkin' about?" Jake was getting impatient with the circles this conversation was going in. *If he's figurin' on puttin' me in the iron-bar hotel, why don't he get on with it?*

"The prints we found appeared to be from new clodhoppers. Not like those run-down, holey wrecks you're wearing. So we set to looking around for more evidence. And guess what, we found some. You surprised?"

"Marshal, nothin' you could say would surprise me. Now, how 'bout you get on with it. I've got business elsewhere."

"All right, all right, just hold your britches. We found a brand new shoe in some brush near the river. Had mud on the sole. Now why would anyone throw away a new piece of footwear like that? Brand spanking new, with your mark on it—but not bought from our local cobbler?"

Jake narrowed his eyes and looked intently at Marshal Gardner. His interest was now piqued. All the dancing around the barn was beginning to make sense.

"Settin' someone up for a crime he didn't commit comes to mind," Jake muttered. He started chewing on his lip.

"Do you have anyone around here that'd like to get you strung up? You must have enemies by the wagonload. Bounty hunters don't usually have a score of friends following them about, singing their praises."

Jake didn't say anything. His mind was awhirl with possibilities, even though no one came to mind at that moment.

"You got anything else?" Jake said, almost incoherently.

"Nope. I'll let you know if we need to speak further on the subject."

Jake left the marshal's office in a thoughtful daze. *Hell, I know I've got enemies, but none of them ever tried to get me hung for somethin' I didn't do. They've always come at me head-on. Of course, none of 'em survived.* He turned down the alleyway toward the corral to saddle his horse for a ride out to the Munder spread.

* * *

When Jake rode up to the ranch house where Teresa Munder lived like a queen, he was immediately struck by the fact that nothing seemed out of place. No wind-blown trash caught in the fence around the chicken coop, no gate needing mended, no shingles needing replaced. The whole ranch looked like it was pristine. Too pristine. That much neatness bothered him, although he wasn't sure why. As he dismounted, the front door flung open and Teresa Munder stood like a China doll in its place.

"Well, Mister Rattlesnake, since you've arrived without my husband in tow, I'd have to say you've failed in your quest."

"No, ma'am. Rattlesnake Jake doesn't fail. At anything. This time is no different. I don't have your husband with me because I figure he's a good hundred miles from here, by now. But, I do need to ask you a couple questions."

"Questions? Like what?"

"I'm wonderin' if you've ever heard of a man named Malchius Offerman."

"Yes, I believe that's the name he gave when he was out here asking about my husband just a few days ago. Why do you ask? Does he have something to do with whatever it is you're not telling me?"

"It's possible. I'm just tryin' to piece it all together."

"So, did my dear husband run off like a whimpering child at not getting his way? Where is he?"

"Like I said, a long way off. Can't say exactly where, but for certain, he's in no shape to return to your lovin' arms."

"Just what are you saying?"

"Don't know any way to say it but to get right to the heart of things, ma'am. Your husband is dead."

Teresa's hand shot to her mouth to cover her shock. Tears began to flow and she seemed to be struggling to remain standing. Her normally rigid stance had taken on a decidedly shaky demeanor. Jake stepped forward to take her by the arm and direct her to one of the rattan chairs in the porch. Unsteadily, she eased onto the plush seat.

"H-how'd he die? Wh-where—?" Her mumbled words came haltingly.

"You really don't want to know, ma'am. He's dead and that's all there is to it. You'll have to accept the facts as they are."

"No! I want to know why he's dead, where he was killed, and who did it! Do you understand me, Mister Bounty Hunter?" she screamed. "You owe me the truth! Five hundred dollars worth of truth."

"Ma'am, I'm just tryin' to spare—"

"Now! All of it!" Her beautiful green eyes were suddenly aflame with an anger that only a grief-stricken woman completely out of control could summon forth.

Teresa's raging demand shoved Jake over the edge to a violation of his own rule—to never burden a lady with the seedy truth of a husband's other life.

"All right, but you ain't gonna like it. He was stabbed to death in a whorehouse in Dogleg City. I'm sorry, but best I can figure out is that his body was then thrown into the river, left to float to who-the-hell-knows-where. If he hasn't already sunk to the bottom, I'd say he's still on his little excursion. Excuse my bluntness, ma'am, but you did ask—er, demand—the truth."

Teresa sat stunned by what she'd just heard. Unable to speak, she stared off into the distance. Jake shifted uneasily from one foot to the other. Having removed his hat as he approached the porch, he now set it back on his head and turned to leave.

"No. Please don't," Teresa said.

"Ma'am? I got nothing more to say."

"I'd like, uh, I mean, would you care to come inside for, uh, a cup of coffee, or—?"

"I reckon I could do that."

"Your honesty has been like a breath of fresh air, Jake. Do you mind if I call you Jake?"

"No ma'am, you can call me anything you'd like."

"Good. Please step inside, out of the sight of any prying eyes of the ranch-hands."

Jake again removed his hat and followed the lady inside. He followed through the parlor, up the stairway, and down a long hallway. She didn't even hesitate as she opened the door to a lavishly decorated bedroom. She walked to the bed, stopped, and began fiddling with something on her dress. When she turned around, he realized she'd unbuttoned the top of it, letting the garment slide from her shoulders. She didn't skip a beat as she unsnapped a bodice, shrugging out of two petticoats, and pulled loose the ribbon that held her long hair. She took one step toward him, placing her hands on his shoulders.

"I know what people say about me, that I'm a cold, frigid woman. That's the impression my husband had, too. But he never tried to find the truth behind the façade. I'm not that way at all." She pulled him down to kiss her.

Jake, never a man to miss a once-in-a-lifetime opportunity, began shucking his clothes like they were full of fire ants. They tumbled onto the thickest, softest mattress he'd ever laid on.

* * *

Late in the day, Jake mounted up for the ride back to town. His confusion as to what had just happened to him whirled around in his muddled, but deliriously happy, brain. Teresa stood in the open door, clad only in a long, satin robe that she held closed at the throat, and gazed after him demurely. He waved and spurred his horse to a trot. He began playing back the events of the day. First he's accused of murder, then he was forced to tell a widow of her husband's grisly demise, and, if that weren't enough excitement for a simple, bounty hunting gunslinger, he was summarily summoned to the greatest pleasure he'd ever known in the arms of the widow herself.

As the sun began its final plunge toward the flat lands beyond, he mulled over the past hours. He first wondered what kind of a man Munder had been. How could he have not really known the lady he was married to? How could any man miss something that was obvious to Jake early on? From the time he first laid eyes on Teresa, he felt a lustful attraction to her; an overwhelming desire to sample what he felt must be beneath that mask of propriety she had tried so hard to wear. She'd succeeded in her subterfuge with the other citizens of Wolf Creek, but how could a woman like that fool the very man she lived with? Or did she? Jake was rapidly coming to the conclusion that Alexander Munder was merely a blind, thickheaded fool. Probably deserved what he got. But why? And what was his connection to Offerman, the man who Abby claimed stabbed him to death? And did Offerman's apparent relationship with Mayor Dab Henry have anything to do with anything? Lots of questions, but damned few answers.

As he reined in behind the Wolf's Den, he stepped down with a strange feeling. Just riding down the street made him uneasy. Something was not right. Folks appeared reluctant to step outside. His curiosity piqued, Jake eased in the back door to the saloon, taking care to look every person he passed in the eye. Quieter than usual, he leaned on the bar and asked the bartender, Mack, what the hell was going on that was making the whole town seem jumpy. Even the house gambler, Preston Vance, seemed off his game. Jake never liked Vance, he couldn't tolerate the phony Southern charm the man exhibited, so he managed to stay away from him. Mack the bartender bent over, looked around nervously, then leaned close to say something.

"Jake, Ira told me to tell you there's a fella upstairs wants to have words with you."

"Who is it, Mack?"

"Gambler from the Lucky Break, Samuel Jones."

Jake scowled. "What the hell does he want?"

Mack was getting shakier by the minute.

"I don't know, Jake," he said. "Ever'body's been talkin' about him, though, since that duel yesterday. I mean hell, we have gunfights all the time, but most folks around here have never seen no fancy by-the-rules duel before."

Jake's eyes narrowed. This was damned shady. First Ira Breedlove puts him on the gambler's scent, now that proposed quarry had shown up at Ira's place wanting to meet.

"He armed?" Jake demanded.

"I'd say so. But I doubt Ira'd send you into a trap." Mack looked around furtively. "Fact is," he whispered, "Ira said to tell you somethin'—'you're welcome,' he said."

So that was it. Ira wanted this fancy duelist dead—the saloon owner had as much as said he'd prefer Jake to just shoot first and find out if the jasper was wanted or not afterwards. It seemed that waiting for replies to Jake's telegrams about reward dodgers was too long a process for Ira. And now he had somehow arranged to hand-deliver him—but Jake doubted the gambler would put his neck on the block like a lamb to the slaughter.

"Your boss has never gone out of his way to be so helpful to me before, Mack. Why today?"

"I dunno, Jake."

"I ought to make you walk into that room ahead of me, Mack. That way, if this gambler shoots, you'll get something extra for helpin' set me up."

"I-I'm sorry, Jake. I don't know what's goin' on, and I don't wanna know."

157

Jake checked his Colt and slowly ascended the stairs. He looked back over his shoulder and asked Mack what room the man was in.

Mack held up three fingers.

When Jake reached room #3, he listened for a second before knocking. He stood aside as he did so.

"Come on in, Jake."

Jake opened the door cautiously, pushing it wide so he could see the man on the overstuffed chair clearly. He didn't seem to have a gun in his hand. In fact, a holster and revolver were wrapped up with a cartridge belt lay on the table next to him. Jake went in. He still didn't recognize the man.

"They told me downstairs you wanted to have a chat," Jake said.

"I do, indeed. Have a seat. And don't be so suspicious. I'm not packing any hideout Derringers this evening." The man held out his hand. Jake shook it, but was, as yet, unconvinced there was no danger. Jones smiled. "No dueling pistols, either," he said.

"What's this all about?"

"I'd like to fill you in on a few things before we get down to business."

Jake nodded.

"Do you remember me?"

"Of course. You're a gambler for Dab Henry. Samuel Jones. I've seen you around. Mack said you plugged a man named Hébert this afternoon. But I don't see what any of that has to do with me."

"It has everything to do with you, my friend."

"I'm all ears. Enlighten me," Jake said.

"Do you know a man named Malchius Offerman?"

"Uh-huh. Whiskey drummer. Fact is, I've been lookin' for him, and I keep missin' him somehow."

"He's looking for you, too. And he doesn't intend to miss you."

"Damn," Jake said. "Abby must've blabbed to him that I was on his scent."

Samuel Jones shook his head. "I'm not sure what you're talking about, or how Abby's involved, but this time you're the prey. Offerman has been on your scent, for some time. He came to Wolf Creek specifically to kill you."

"Kill me? I told you, I never met the man."

"Yes, but you met his brother. He'd been in on a bank robbery in Austin where some teller were shot. You tracked him down to St. Joe and killed him for the bounty—Offerman said his name was Clyde."

Jake's eyes lit in recognition. "Yeah. Clyde Offerman in St. Joe. One of them tellers was the mayor's son, and the whole town pitched in for the reward. That's why the name sounded so damn familiar—I just never would've connected him with a whiskey drummer. I remember the wily bastard somehow got behind me and started throwin' lead. Got me in the leg before I was able to bring him down. Hated havin' to kill him, but it was him or me. Unfortunately, the reward was cut in half because I brought back a body instead of a candidate for a necktie party. The town was lookin' forward to havin' its revenge and figured I stole it from them. His brother!"

Jake's expression went from recognition to surprise and finally to a seething rage, all in the time it might take a man to blink. He pushed himself up from the chair.

"I'll be damned," Jake said. "This whiskey peddler killed that Laird fella and framed me for it. And just in case that didn't work, he killed Teresa Munder's husband for apparently no good reason—but really it was on the gamble she'd hire me to go lookin' when he never came home, and the trail would lead me to Offerman. I don't understand why he'd do that part, though."

It seemed Samuel Jones wasn't through with him. Not by a damned sight.

"Hold on, Jake, there's more. Sit down and hear me out."

Jake took a minute to decide whether to listen or to go after Offerman without delay. But, after a moment, he did return to the seat he'd just vacated. "Give," he said.

"Offerman's got himself three hired guns signed on to help him take you down. Maybe more, by now. I'd wager that's why he killed that blowhard Munder—so you'd come straight to him, not realizing he'd rounded up enough killers to make it a trap."

Jake stared hard at the gambler. "How the hell do you know so much about all this, anyways?"

Samuel Jones smiled. "The duel. It got Offerman's attention, and he approached me this morning offering to buy my gun. To help kill you. In fact, he's waiting for me to join him at the Lucky Break now, and we're supposed to wait for you to show up."

"And you decided instead to come tell me the whole story? What's in it for you?"

Jones stared back. "I asked if you remembered me, earlier. I didn't mean, do you know who I am—of course you do, we've both been in this town long enough for that. I meant, do you remember me from the barricades. When the Kiowa attacked Wolf Creek."

Jake cocked his head. "I recall you was there, sure."

"So you don't remember. Well, I do, and I won't forget."

"You lost me, *amigo*."

"We were at the barricade," the gambler explained. "A Kiowa brave got the better of me—he seemed to just drop out of the sky—and he was about to dash my brains out with a tomahawk. Then you tackled him, and stuck him with that Arkansas toothpick of yours."

Jake grunted. "Sounds kinda familiar. But I believe I killed a bunch of Injuns that day, it all kinda runs together."

"Maybe you did," Jones said. "But that was the only one who was a hair's breadth from killing me. I am a man of honor, Jake. In fact, my honor is the only thing I really have managed to hold onto in this life. And I never forget a debt like that."

Jake nodded. "Well, if you say so. Makes sense to me, believe it or not. So I'm much obliged, and you can consider us even. Now if you'll excuse me, I'm fixin' to go kill me a drummer."

"A man'd be foolish to call Offerman out without someone to watch his back," Samuel Jones said.

"Is that an offer?" Jake asked, hesitant.

"A debt this big is not canceled just because you say it is—and a simple warning won't do. You saved my life, now I'm standing with you and backing your play."

Jake had never felt the need for someone to watch out for him, but if what Jones claimed was true, he was facing odds of four-to-one at best. It might be worth it to make certain he didn't ride past Teresa Munder's ranch in an undertaker's coach with a bullet in his back. He rubbed his stubbly chin and broke into a wry grin, both at the thought of seeing Teresa again, as well as having an extra gun as he went up against a cold-blooded murderer. He suddenly reached a hand across to Samuel Jones.

"Mister Jones, you've got yourself a deal. When do you want to start this soiree?"

"Now seems as good a time as any."

Jake laughed heartily. "I'll be damned," he said. "It's gonna break old Ira's heart to see us walk out of here together!"

"Why's that?"

"Because he wanted *me* to kill *you*. I'm not sure why. I think it was just to annoy your boss."

The gambler shook his head. "This is a hell of a town."

* * *

It was dusk when they arrived at the Lucky Break. Piano music and laughter rolled out over the batwing doors. Malchius Offerman's horse was at the hitching post. Rattlesnake Jake paused before he stepped up onto the boardwalk.

"Samuel," he said, "why don't you go around back and slip in the back way. He'll likely have anyone he's hired to back him up close-by, in case I show up before you do. I'm sure he knows by now that Abby has let it slip that I'm lookin' to take him in for the murder of Alexander Munder. And he probably has figured out that his plot to get me hanged for killing Laird what's-his-name has fallen short, since Marshal Gardner hasn't put me in shackles, yet. He'll be ready for a confrontation."

"Give me a few minutes to get inside. Then, make your appearance. I'll back you," Sam said.

Jake waited briefly, knowing Sam wouldn't dawdle on his way to get in on the action. As he pushed open the batwings, he saw Offerman sitting at a table with three other men. Although he'd never personally met Offerman, he knew instantly which one of the three he was. Malchius Offerman was a dead ringer for his deceased brother, the man Jake had killed in Missouri. He kept his hand on the butt of his Colt as he approached the table.

"Malchius Offerman?"

"That's me," the drummer said. Although he dressed like a salesman, he didn't hold himself like one, somehow. He seemed very calm and confident, and dangerous. "I didn't catch your name," Offerman added.

"Oh, you know my name," Jake said. "You've been doin' your best to get me accused of a murder I didn't commit."

"I've got no idea what the hell you're talking about, mister. Why don't you just move on before my friends and I take umbrage at your accusations." Offerman let his hand slip beneath the table.

One of his companions was a portly, unwashed man. The second was a Mexican with a thick beard. The third one Jake recognized from the Wolf's Den, a lay-about named Randolph. They all slowly scooted their chairs back from the table. The other patrons had seen this show before; the chatter stopped. Boomduck Gentry, the vulture-faced piano player, ended his song abruptly with a single discordant chord.

"Why did you kill Alexander Munder, Offerman?"

"Who says I did?"

"Abby, the madam."

Offerman chuckled, without mirth. "Well, since you ask, have you ever laid eyes on Munder's widow? I figure to have myself a little romp with the lady, as soon as our business here is finished. I'd heard plenty of talk about how controlling she is—I figured when he didn't come home she'd send someone to look for him, or for his killer, and that you'd be the first one folks would send

163

her to. And then we'd have this very meeting—but I knew she wouldn't do it right off, so I'd have time to prepare for you."

"And pluggin' Laird? That was to set me up to take the fall?"

"Of course. That was plan A. Then, if you wriggled out of that, plan B would still get your attention. But I figure you know what this is really all about by now, don't you?"

"Uh-huh. You're upset that I had to put a bullet in that murderin' pile of manure you called a brother. Right?"

The Mexican's shoulder moved, just a hair, and Samuel Jones called out from the back of the room.

"Hold on, amigo," the gambler said. "The odds aren't as good as you think."

Offerman scowled. "Jones," he hissed. "I was wondering where you were. You're an idiot, he can't pay you half what I would've."

"He already has," Jones said.

The other customers had quickly made their way outside, and Rob Parker had set down his whiskey glasses and ducked behind the bar. Dab Henry stepped out of his office, saw what was happening, and quickly went back inside.

Rattlesnake Jake smiled coldly. "Go ahead, gents, yank those smoke wagons, if you've a mind to."

Offerman's hand shot to his revolver as he jumped up. His face was red with rage. He'd no more than gotten the six-shooter out of his holster than he saw a smoky blast coming his way. Malchius Offerman had but a split second to appraise his situation before falling back into his chair, a bloody bloom spreading across his white shirt, with a bullet hole in the center of it. As he dropped back with a thud, his gun went off, blowing a hole in his own boot. He was stone cold dead.

The other men had leapt to their feet and drawn as well. Randolph flipped the table over and dove to the ground behind it, pulling his Colt as he did so. The Mexican whirled around and raised his gun at Samuel Jones—the gambler stood sideways to make a harder target, his revolver leveled, and sent a bullet crashing into the Mexican's forehead.

The fat man snapped off a shot at Jake, terrified, and the bullet whizzed past the bounty hunter's ear. Jake pumped three bullets rapidly into the man's chest, and he whimpered as he collapsed on the saloon floor.

Randolph fired at Samuel Jones, and the slug clipped the gambler's jacket. Jones returned fire, hitting the crouching gunman in the gut. Randolph struggled to lift his gun for another shot, and a second bullet from Jones punched into his heart. He sagged into a heap with a final gasp.

It was over. Ten shots had been fired. Six seconds had passed. Four men lay dead in pools of blood on the floor around the overturned table. Gun smoke hung thick in the air, and curled from the pistol barrels of Rattlesnake Jake and Samuel Jones. Rob Parker slowly raised his head above the bar.

Jake heard deliberate footsteps behind him, and he turned slowly.

Marshal Sam Gardner stood in the doorway, leaning on the cane in his left hand, his right hand resting on his revolver's butt. His deputies, Quint Croy and Seamus O'Connor, flanked him.

A moment passed in silence, then the marshal spoke.

"Well, then," he said. "Are you boys about finished here, or did you plan to shoot one another a few times while you're at it?"

"That's up to Jake, I guess," Jones said. Then, to the bounty hunter, he added, "Now we're square. If you want to take Ira up on his offer."

Rattlesnake Jake slowly lowered his weapon and eased it into his holster.

"No," he said, "we ain't square. Now it's swung back to you. If some other New Orleans dandy shows up sniffin' around, I reckon I'll be backin' you up. It may be hard for you to believe, but I do know something about honor myself."

"There's not any wanted posters on Mister Jones here down at the sheriff's office," Gardner offered. "So he's not wanted in Kansas. What some rich family in New Orleans wants is none of my business, unless it causes trouble in my town."

"That's good enough for me," Jake said. He had privately decided to tell Dave Maynard at the telegraph office to just thrown away whatever answers he received to his inquiries about Samuel Jones.

Jones holstered his own weapon. "Much obliged, I believe, is the appropriate response."

Jake shrugged. "I figure it's in my best interests to just keep you around—if there're any private bounties on you, I'll have you handy if I ever have a dry month and need some quick cash."

They nodded politely at one another, then Jake turned to the sheriff. "You need to question us, or any of that?"

Gardner shook his head. "No, boys, I guess I have a pretty good idea what happened. You're free to go."

"Good," Jake said. "I have business."

"Where are you headed?" Samuel Jones asked.

"On a sad mission, I'm afraid," Jake said with a wry smile. "I have to go out to the Munder ranch to let the widow know we got her husband's killer. Then, I'll probably have to hang around awhile consoling the poor, distraught thing. Could take a spell."

Jake walked through the door. Gardner spoke to his deputies.

"Quint, go fetch Gravely. Tell him to bring his wagon. Seamus, grab some of those yay-hoos out there and stack these bodies up in the street."

Jones took a seat at his regular table.

Dab Henry's door cautiously opened once more, and His Honor stuck his head out.

"It's safe, Dab," Gardner said, "but let's just step into your office and have a conversation, shall we?"

Dab nodded absently, and Gardner walked in and closed the door behind him.

"Dab," he said, "looks like you're gonna have to get a new whiskey representative. We seem to go through 'em quick around here."

"I—yeah, I guess so."

"I also think you're gonna have to level with me for once," the marshal said. "About your pal Mister Offerman."

Dab sighed. "Hell, Sam," he said. "I didn't know all of this was gonna happen. Hell."

Gardner sat down in the mayor's guest chair, and put his bad leg up on Dab's desk.

"Keep talkin'," he said.

"Well," Dab said nervously, "I'm not sure where to start." He sounded like a child caught at the cookie jar.

"Just jump in anywhere," Gardner said.

Dab sighed. "It all started when that Laird Jenkins character started coming around. He was in here Monday night, drinkin' maybe a little more than he planned on, and he started talking to Offerman. He told the drummer about how him and Ira Breedlove was *compadres* from way back, and how good Ira had been to him, givin' him work and all when he came into town."

"What kind of work?" the marshal asked, although he knew.

"He was workin' on Asa Pepper," Dab said. "Ira was gonna float that old bastard a loan, in order to get a piece of his action and start squeezin' me out. That made me mad as hell, I don't mind sayin'—it's just not honest business."

"In other words, you didn't think of it first," the marshal said, and the mayor shrugged.

"Anyways," Dab continued, "the drummer came to me right away with this information. And he said he could help me—if I promised to give him my exclusive whiskey buyin' business, he'd throw a wrench in Ira's little plan. So I thought, sure, why not."

Gardner took out a cigar and lit it. "Naturally, you never inquired into how he was going to disrupt Ira's operation. Or whether those methods would be legal."

"I sure didn't think he would shoot Jenkins in the back while he was takin' a leak," the mayor said ruefully.

"Not that you cared," Gardner pointed out, and Dab shrugged again.

"All right, then," the marshal said. "Let me see if I have all this straight. You authorize a whiskey drummer to gum up Ira's plan to convince Asa Pepper to help him drive you and the other saloons out of the whore business. The whiskey drummer accomplishes this by murdering the joker who is probably the closest thing Ira has ever had to a friend, including his dog. Am I right so far?"

"Well, I wouldn't put it quite that way, but basically, yeah."

"So then Ira is very unhappy. This Frenchman Hébert comes along looking for your house gambler, gets himself shot, and Ira figures Samuel Jones must have a price on his head. So—from what those boys were saying outside—Ira puts our local bounty hunter on Jones, mostly as a way to send you a message."

"Message?"

"That he knows you were behind his friend's murder, and he was going to make you pay. Probably a piece at a time."

"Well, that seems childish on his part," Dab said. Gardner ignored him.

"But the joke was on you and Ira," the marshal continued, "because the whiskey drummer was playing you both, and everybody else—all to get at Rattlesnake Jake. Which he got his chance at, but he didn't do so good. Offerman was pretty slick, but criminal enterprise seemed to be a little harder than he thought it would be."

Gardner puffed on the cigar and blew a smoke ring, then said, "I have to admit, though, he did pretty damn good at the *selling* part. He sold all you sons of bitches, and good. The facing down two gunfighters, that he didn't handle well at all. There's a lesson to be learned in there somewhere, Dab, if we can figure out what it is."

"You really think so?" Dab said, a little confused.

"Nah, not really. But here's what I *do* think. Our murderer is dead as hell, so that's a positive outcome. As for everything else I've said, well, most of it is conjecture

169

and not one whit of it would hold up in court. So here's the situation I'm left with—you and Ira Breedlove are pulling people's strings, and sending people to kill each other, all so you can prove which one's got the biggest horns."

He puffed again, then turned his head and blew smoke straight at the mayor.

"Not much I can do about it, I guess," Gardner said. "Not this time. But you idiots are gonna keep pushing each other, harder and harder, till you blow the lid off this town. And when it gets to that point, percentages or not, if I have to I'll just shoot you both."

Gardner stood up, with some difficulty—his leg had stiffened on him. He cocked his head, listening to the muffled noise from the main room.

"Sounds like your business is pickin' up, Dab," he said. "And that's damn good news. I don't want to cut my own purse, not if I can help it. You have a good night, now. I'm headed over to the Wolf's Den to tell Ira the same thing I just told you."

"You wouldn't—you wouldn't really do that, would you?"

"Wouldn't what, tell Ira for sure that you were behind his friend Laird's murder?"

"No," Dab said. "I mean, you wouldn't really shoot me, would you?"

Sam Gardner smiled. "I suppose I'd probably shoot Ira first, if that makes you feel better."

Dab paused a moment. "It does, kinda," he said.

Gardner opened the door and stepped into the saloon. Quint Croy was waiting for him.

"We got those bodies over to Gravely's," Quint said.

"Good, good. Let them soak his floorboards for awhile."

"Marshal?" Quint said.

"Yeah?"

Quint looked confused. "Marshal, I'm not sure I understand everything that has happened this week."

Gardner put an arm on his deputy's shoulder as they passed through the batwings and into the Kansas night.

"Not much to understand, really," Sam said. "Just another night in Dogleg City, that's all."

Marshal Sam Gardner paused and looked around the dark street, smiling almost sadly. "Just another night in Dogleg City."

THE END

ABOUT THE AUTHORS

PHIL DUNLAP

I am the author of nine published Westerns, with three more in the "chute". I've contributed to three anthologies, and published numerous short stories. I write chiefly in the Western genre, although I confess to harboring a soft spot for mysteries. Most of my Westerns are also mysteries as a number of reviewers have pointed out. *Saving Mattie* (Treble Heart Books) won the EPPIE Award for the Best Traditional Western 2009. *Blood on the Rimrock* (Avalon Books, now AmazonEncore) was a finalist in the 2009 Best Books of Indiana competition sponsored by the Indiana State Library and the Library of Congress.

I am a longtime journalist and freelance writer living in Carmel, IN. I was a newspaper correspondent for several years for a large daily newspaper before turning to writing novels full-time.

JERRY GUIN

I was born in Arkansas then migrated to the high country in Idaho and now live on the edge of Big Foot country in

Northern California. My wife Ginny proofreads and coaches everything I write. I've always lived in or near the woods, so it was no surprise to friends and family when my first book, *Matsutake Mushroom,* a nature guidebook, was printed in 1997. Since then I have written 28 articles and western short stories for various magazines such as *Western Digest, The Shootist, Roundup* and others. I have stories in several western anthologies and my novel *Drover's Vendetta* was released in 2011.

After I became a member of Western Fictioneers, the organization provided plenty of new opportunities for me to write alongside some of the best western authors in the business. I now have stories in *The Traditional West, Six-Guns and Slay Bells, A Creepy Cowboy Christmas* and the first chapter of Wolf Creek book 3, *Murder in Dogleg City.*

MATTHEW P. MAYO

My short stories have been nominated for the Spur Award and Peacemaker Award, and appear in a variety of anthologies, including *Six-Guns and Slay Bells*, *Beat to a Pulp*, *Out of the Gutter*, Moonstone Books anthologies, and the DAW Books anthologies *Timeshares* and *Steampunk'd*.

My novels include the Westerns *Winters' War*; *Wrong Town (Roamer, Book 1)*; *Hot Lead, Cold Heart*; *Dead Man's Ranch*; and *Tucker's Reckoning*, and I write for a popular series of "all-action" Westerns. My critically acclaimed non-fiction books include *Cowboys, Mountain*

Men & Grizzly Bears; Bootleggers, Lobstermen & Lumberjacks; Sourdoughs, Claim Jumpers & Dry Gulchers; and *Haunted Old West.*

My wife, photographer Jennifer Smith-Mayo, and I operate Gritty Press (www.GrittyPress.com), the flying spin-kick of the publishing world, and can frequently be found roving the highways and byways of the West with our wee pup, Nessie. Drop by my e-ranch for a cuppa mud and a chinwag at www.MatthewMayo.com.

CHUCK TYRELL

I was born and raised in Arizona and worked stock and farmed until I ran away to college and never went back. I decided I wanted to make my living as a writer in 1975. Up until that time, I'd been a marketing and advertising person. I took a correspondence course on writing for magazines, and sold my first article in 1976, when I was working at a newspaper and DJ-ing on nighttime radio at the same time. Since that first sale, I've had very few articles turned down. Now, of course, I write them only on assignment. Also in 1976, I won the Editor and Publisher Magazine award for the best direct mail campaign for a small newspaper in the United States.By 1977, I earned my entire living with my typewriter, writing ads, annual reports, newsletters, magazine articles, and sometimes a newspaper article.

I've read westerns all my life. The first one I remember was Smokey, by Will James. I read everything I could find, living far away from the west in Japan. In 1979, I wrote a western novel for a Louis L'Amour write-alike contest. Didn't win. Decided I could not write fiction. The typewritten manuscript occupied a bottom desk drawer until 2000. I dusted it off and edited it as I input it into a computer file. Sent it off to a publisher, Robert Hale Ltd., in London. They bought it providing I'd cut it down to 40,000 words. The novel is now known as *Vulture Gold*, the first of the Havelock novels.

Besides awards in advertising and article writing, a short story won the 2010 Oaxaca International Literature Competition and my novel *The Snake Den* won the 2011 Global eBook Award for western fiction. Other than that, I just write westerns and fantasy. My home is in Japan, where I live with one wife and one dog and one father-in-law, visited quite often by daughters and grandkids. I write most of my fiction by longhand, usually at Starbucks. Other writing I do on the laptop. My website is www.chucktyrell.com and my blog is www.chucktyrell-outlawjournal.blogspot.com I have a number of short stories lying around in various anthologies.

L. J. (LIVIA J.) WASHBURN

I have been writing award-winning, critically acclaimed mysteries, westerns, romances, and historical novels for thirty years. I began to write in collaboration with my husband, author James Reasoner, and soon branched out into telling my own stories. We have had a long career working together, tweaking and editing each others stories. I live in the Texas countryside with James, one of my two daughters, and my dogs. Even though I have an office, I do most of my writing in our living room sitting in a recliner with a laptop perched on the arm of the chair and two small Chihuahua/ Min Pins in my lap. It's a great life. My website is www.liviawashburn.com, and my blog is http://liviajwashburn.blogspot.com.

TROY D. SMITH

I am from the Upper Cumberland region of Tennessee. My work has appeared in many anthologies, and in journals such as *Louis L'Amour Western Magazine, Civil War Times,* and *Wild West.* In addition, I've written novels in several genres—from mysteries like *Cross Road Blues* to the Civil War epic *Good Rebel Soil.* My other Civil War epic, *Bound for the Promise-Land,* won a Spur Award in 2001 and I was a finalist on two other occasions. Two of my short stories are finalists for this year's Peacemaker Award for western fiction. In a massive lapse of collective judgment, the membership of Western Fictioneers elected me president for 2012. I received my Ph.D. from the University of Illinois, and teach American Indian history at Tennessee Tech. My motto is: "I don't write about things that happen to people, I write about people that things happen to." My website is www.troyduanesmith.com , and my blog is http://tnwordsmith.blogspot.com

The Wolf Creek series:

Book 1: Bloody Trail
Book 2: Kiowa Vengeance
Book 3: Murder in Dogleg City
Book 4: The Taylor County War

More to come!

Also available from Western Fictioneers:

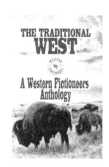 

www.westernfictioneers.com

Western Fictioneers

Made in the USA
Coppell, TX
26 February 2023

13451044R10098